COMMAND TO GIVE THANKS ALL THE YEAR ROUND

(DAILY DEVOTIONAL)

~ GIVE THANKS ALL THE YEAR ROUND ~

Dorcas Akinleyimu

~ GIVE THANKS ALL THE YEAR ROUND ~

COPYRIGHT AND PUBLISHER'S PAGE
Command To Give Thanks All The Year Round. The
First Edition 2022 All Rights Reserved
Copyright @ 2022 Dorcas Akinleyimu

ISBN 978-0-578-34322-8

The scripture quotations used in this book are taken from different
versions of the Holy Bible used with permission. Some scriptures in this
book were repeated in several places for emphasis.

Cover Design by
Bliss & Fire Network Publications, Garland, Texas Email:
info@blissandfire.com
Tel: 1-800-930-0547

TABLE OF CONTENTS

~ GIVE THANKS ALL THE YEAR ROUND ~

DEDICATION

This Daily Devotion is dedicated to this generation and the next as we all create quality and quantity time in our daily quiet time with the Lord, our God. Amen.

FOREWORD

Many people believe in God. Some of them live their lives with great expectations from Him. Others do holy things for God. Some people love God and serve Him. While many long for more blessings, divine provisions, and protection, yet not being grateful.

In this devotional book, Pastor Dorcas uses her experience in walking with God to encourage every individual to live a daily life of thanksgiving and expression of gratitude to God for the simplest blessings in our lives. Amid the

~ GIVE THANKS ALL THE YEAR ROUND ~

daily struggles, let us occasionally stop to take a deep breath and "let everything that has breath praise the LORD" (Psalm 150:6). Giving thanks always unto God will strengthen your relationship with Him, and He will reciprocate with more abundant blessings.

~ Pastor Jude Folorunso Akinleyimu (M. A., Theology)

ACKNOWLEDGEMENT

To God be all praise and worship for all He had done, which no man can do. Jehovah, the all-wise, all-knowing, and understanding Father, I appreciate you, Father God, the Son — Jesus Christ, and the Holy Spirit for your love over my life. To you be all the glory. I also appreciate God for His leading and guidance. I appreciate my family, husband, and children — their spouses and all my grandkids for their help, support, and encouragement.

~ GIVE THANKS ALL THE YEAR ROUND ~

I felt the power of answered prayers offered for my husband and me through our family/home church, Christian Faith and Fellowship Mission Int'l, and especially Sanctuary of Praise. The Lord is your rewarder and will greatly reward your labor of love.

I also appreciate Pastors Wales and Rita Goriola, who encouraged me to make the pamphlet like a daily devotional and help publish the book. Thanks to you both.

I want everyone who will read or skim through this book and take the challenge as I have done. Take up the challenge to listen and obey by heeding to the Holy Spirit in all you do as Christians. I encourage all readers to give thanks to God in all areas of life and any situation; good

10

~ GIVE THANKS ALL THE YEAR ROUND ~

times, bad times, joyful times, sorrowful times, trial times, and even amidst challenges. In all things, keep on saying, "THANK YOU, JESUS."

INTRODUCTION

At the end of 2016, my husband received a cylinder of cookies about 25.5cm long from his place of work during Christmas time. When we tasted the cookies, they were too sweet. So, we decided to trash the cookies and recycle the can—as I was about to put the can in a recycle bin, the Spirit of the Lord spoke to me to STOP!

Although I stopped, I didn't listen. I continue to make an attempt to put the can into the recycle bin. The Spirit of the Lord spoke to me again to

~ GIVE THANKS ALL THE YEAR ROUND ~

STOP, then I stopped, and I listened. He then said to me, "Use this Jar to write Thank You Jesus every day as you start the New Year." Then I said, Lord, I thank you for allowing me to listen to you, and I promised that I would obey. I cleaned the can and placed a Golden ribbon on top of the lid. On January 1st, 2017, the journey started.

I thanked God that He had not allowed me to disobey. I met a lot of challenges, but God helped me and saw me through. Some of the days throughout the year, evil things popped up, accidents happened, and some bad news was received. But the Spirit of the Lord continues to remind me to say, "Thank You, Jesus."

~ GIVE THANKS ALL THE YEAR ROUND ~

At the end of the year 2017, specifically on Christmas Day, I shared the "Everyday Thank You Jesus" testimony that the Lord has commanded me and read a few of the notes written in the Jar with my family. We were about six in number and discussed some of the things written throughout the year. Then one of my daughters said, "What are you going to do with all these pieces of paper? Trash them." I immediately responded, No! I will not trash them. I will keep them in the Jar. My daughter-in-law now said, "I can help you put them together neatly and make a book out of it." That sounded amazing to me, so I took some time to organize the notes in chronological order by days and months. My daughter-in-law typed out all the notes I arranged for her and created the book. She did a good job, and may the Lord himself bless her abundantly. Amen

At the close of 2017, the Spirit of the Lord told me that this assignment is for three years. So, the following year, which was 2018 and 2019, I kept writing "Everyday Thank You Jesus," knowing that God wants to do something great.

The first book came out as a pamphlet, which we distributed during our second annual women's conference in July 2018.

So, by the end of 2018, I did not stop writing until the end of the third year, which was 2019. FOR THREE YEARS, all I wrote every day has been summarized to become a daily devotional. A pastor family friend with his wife encouraged me to make it a daily devotional booklet. I will talk more about them later.

Please read, enjoy, learn something, always listen to the Holy Spirit and be obedient to him. Most of the things written are personal, but I am not ashamed to share them. The three years have been summed up to become what it is today. May the Lord bless the readers abundantly.

There are 365 days in each of these three years, which means we did not have February 29th. So, the Lord said, on February 29th, just say, "Thank You, Jesus, for Leap Year."

My "Thank You Jesus" notes cover all days of the year, even leap year. As I understand it, God wants me to give him thanks all the days of my

~ GIVE THANKS ALL THE YEAR ROUND ~

life, whether leap year or not. That sounds funny, right? Yes, we just have to thank God for everything, small or big, good or bad. In all things, give thanks. (1 Thessalonians 5:18)

JANUARY

Happy new year, it's our year of God's promises to be fulfilled in our lives. Celebrate Jesus Christ, and you will be celebrated.

JANUARY 1

PRAISE GOD! PRAISE JESUS!

Deuteronomy 26:19

And to make thee high above all nations which He has made, in praise, and in name and in honor; and that thou mayest be an Holy people unto the LORD thy God, as He has spoken.

PRAISE THE HOLY SPIRIT!
It's another brand new year. Thanking you, Lord, for another year for It's our year of elevation, dominion, and victory celebration. No matter what happens this year, it shall turn around in our favor. Amen.

JANUARY 2

Deuteronomy 28:12

The LORD shall open unto thee His good treasure, the heaven to give the rain unto thy land in His season, and to bless all the work of thine hand: and thou shall lend unto many nations, and thou shall not borrow.

Let us thank God for He shall open unto us His good treasure, the heavens will give us rain at its season, the works of our hands He shall bless, and this year, we shall not borrow but lend. Amen.

JANUARY 3

Jeremiah 31:3

*The LORD has appeared of old unto me, saying, yea,
I have love thee with an everlasting love: therefore
with loving kindness have I drawn thee.*

Thanking the Lord for loving us with His
everlasting love, He hath drawn us unto
Himself with loving-kindness. All this year and
beyond, we shall not depart from His presence.
Praise the Lord.

JANUARY 4

Psalm 100:1-2

Make a joyful noise unto the LORD, all ye lands. Serve the LORD with gladness: come before His presence with singing.

We give thanks to you, Lord, we will serve you all our lives with gladness, and surely we will always come to your presence with singing. We started the year joyfully, and we shall end it joyfully.

~ GIVE THANKS ALL THE YEAR ROUND ~

JANUARY 5

Psalm 145:3

Great is the LORD, and greatly to be praised; and His greatness is unsearchable.

Worthy are you, oh LORD, and Great is our God. We will praise you because your greatness is unsearchable.

JANUARY 6

Psalm 106:1

Praise ye the LORD. O give thanks unto the LORD; for He is good: for His mercy endureth for ever.

Let us give God Praise. Let us give thanks unto the LORD. Why? Because He is good, and His mercy is from everlasting to everlasting.

JANUARY 7

Psalm 106:2

Who can utter the mighty acts of the LORD? Who can shew forth all His praise.

As for me, I will utter the mighty acts of the Lord, and I will show forth His praise. Lift up your hands and praise Him. Thank you, Jesus!

JANUARY 8

Psalm 146:1

Praise ye the LORD. Praise the LORD, O my soul.

Hallelujah to the Almighty God. Let our soul
praise the Lord and everything in us, give
thanks to Him.

JANUARY 9

Psalm 105:1

O give thanks unto the LORD; call upon His Name:
make known His deeds among the people.

Great is your name, and you're great to be
worshipped. Hallelujah! We will call upon your
name throughout the year, and we shall make
known Your deeds among the people.

JANUARY 10

Psalm 150:1

Praise ye the LORD. Praise God in His Sanctuary: praise Him in the firmament of His power.

Worthy are you, Lord. Thank you, blessed be your name. We shall praise you in our homes, at your sanctuary, and also in the firmament of your power.

JANUARY 11

Psalm 150:2

*Praise Him for His mighty acts: praise Him
according to His excellent greatness.*

Praise and adoration be unto you our King and
our Maker. We are praising you according to
the excellence of your greatness and for your
mighty actions.

JANUARY 12

Romans 6:17

But God be thanked, that ye were the servants of sin, but ye have obeyed from the heart that form of doctrine which was delivered you.

Let's give thanks to our Awesome God. You're worthy of our praise. We thank you for your unfailing love, thanking you because we are no more the servant of sin.

JANUARY 13

Psalm 77:14

Thou art the God that doest wonders: thou hast declared thy strength among the people.

Let's sing this song to declare the strength of our God among His people: "You're worthy oh, Lord! Invisible God and miracle worker You're worthy oh, Lord!".

JANUARY 14

Psalm 135:5

For I know that the LORD is great, and that our Lord is above all gods.

Lord! You are greater than the greatest, and you're Lord above all gods. Thank you, Jesus.

JANUARY 15

Psalm 7:17

I will praise the LORD according to His Righteousness: and I will sing praise to the Name of the LORD Most High.

Father, we cannot thank you enough for you're worthy of our thanksgiving. And we shall sing praise to your name.

JANUARY 16

Psalm 146:2

While I live will I praise the LORD: I will sing praises unto my God while I have any being.

Glory be to God Almighty for His awesomeness and faithfulness. For being alive, I will praise you more.

JANUARY 17

Psalm 113:5

Who is like unto the LORD our God, who dwelleth on high.

Who is like unto thee Lord, glorious in holiness and fearful in praise? Our God that dwelleth on high, we give you thanks.

JANUARY 18

Psalm 8:1

O LORD our Lord, how excellent is thy Name in all the earth! Who hast set thy glory above the heavens.

Excellent are your works and words of promise to mankind. You set thy glory above the heavens. Whoa! We hope on you, Lord, we rest on your promises, and so we're grateful.

JANUARY 19

Genesis 28:16

And Jacob awaked out of his sleep, and he said,
Surely the LORD is in this place; and I knew it not.

Glory and adoration be unto you our Lord, we
slept well and woke up great. It's your doing,
oh Lord. Thank you for the gift of sleeping and
waking.

JANUARY 20

James 5:16

Confess your faults one to another and pray one for another, that ye may be healed. The effectual fervent prayer of a righteous man availeth much.

Thank you, Lord, for the total and perfect health you gave us as we pray for one another and confess our faults. We love you, Father, and we praise You.

JANUARY 21

Psalm 8:6.

Thou madest him to have dominion over the works of thy hands; thou hast put all things under his feet:

We give you praise, Lord, for putting all things under our feet, including all those that hate us. Thank you, Lord.

JANUARY 22

Psalm 9:1

I will praise thee, O LORD, with my whole heart; I will shew forth all thy marvelous works.

I will praise thee oh, Lord with my whole heart. Let us lavish Him with our praise and bless His name forever. We will praise Him with our whole heart, not by our lips alone, and we will show forth all His marvelous works.

JANUARY 23

Psalm 9:2

I will be glad and rejoice in thee: I will sing praise to thy name, O thou most High.

I am glad and rejoice in you, singing praises to your name for you're excellent and gracious.

JANUARY 24

Psalm 9:11

Sing praises to the LORD, which dwelleth in Zion: declare among the people His doings.

Singing praises to you Lord, You that dwell in Zion, who also lives in us for our hearts had been given unto you. We will declare your loving-kindness among the people of the earth. Receive our praise, dear Lord.

JANUARY 25

Psalm 16:6

The lines are fallen unto me in pleasant places; yea, I have a goodly heritage.

Thank you, Jesus. The Lines are falling unto me in pleasant places, and I have a goodly heritage. What are lines and heritage? They are an idiomatic expression of God's goodness and blessings that He had bestowed upon us.

JANUARY 26

Isaiah 43:25

I, even I, am he that BLOTTETH out thy transgressions for mine own sake, and will not remember thy sins.

Thank you, Jesus! Our Lord and Savior for blotting out our sins and transgression for your name's sake. Please thank Him for His love.

JANUARY 27

Isaiah 43:25

I, even I, am he that blotteth out thy transgressions for mine own sake and will not REMEMBER thy sins.

Thank you, Lord, for remembering my sins no more and keeping me safe from them all.

Hallelujah! Glory!

JANUARY 28

Acts 17:28

For in him we live, and move, and have our being; ...,
For we are also His offspring.

Thank you, Father God, for pouring your Spirit,
Mercy, and Grace upon us as your offspring,
making us live and move in you.

JANUARY 29

Psalm 44:5

Through thee will we push down our enemies:
through thy name will we tread them under that rise
up against us.

Thank you, Abba Father, our Rock of Ages, for
there is none beside You. You push down our
enemies both at home and abroad. Through
your name, we tread them under our feet. We
give you the honor.

JANUARY 30

Psalm 98:4-5

*Make a joyful noise unto the LORD, all the earth:
make a loud noise and rejoice and sing praise. Sing
unto the LORD with the harp; with the harp, and
the voice of a Psalm.*

Thank you, Jesus, our God is good. Let us
praise the Lord together and make a joyful
noise unto Him. Let us sing with harp and clap
our hands and say — Hallow be thy Name.

JANUARY 31

Philippians 4:20

Now unto God and our Father be glory for ever and ever. Amen.

Today, we thank our loving heavenly Father for our families, siblings, friends, stable jobs, good health, and divine healing. It's the last day of the month, we say thank you, Lord. It has only been You.

FEBRUARY

February is the month of love, celebrating the legacy of Valentine. How he embraced and shared the love of God during his own time. You too can leave a good legacy behind. Show the love of Christ to people around you all days of this month. You can do it, and I can do it. May the Lord Almighty helps us.

FEBRUARY 1

John 6:11

And Jesus took the loaves; and when he had given thanks, he distributed to the disciples, and the disciples to them that were set down; and likewise of the fishes as much as they would.

Thank you, Jesus. Giving thanks to God for seeing the beginning of another month. We shall not beg for bread!

FEBRUARY 2

I John 4:8

He that loveth not knoweth not God; for God is love.

Truly, God is love, and love is of God. Your love for mankind is stronger than the blowing of the wind. Praise the Lord, thank you, Jesus, for your love that abideth with us.

FEBRUARY 3

3 John 2

Beloved, I wish above all things that thou mayest prosper and be in health, even as thy soul prospereth.

Thank you, Jesus, everyone that is sick is healed in the name of Jesus, both at home, at the hospital, and in nursing homes. Yes! Amen.

FEBRUARY 4

Psalm 99:1

The LORD reigneth; let the people tremble; He sitteth between the cherubims; let the earth be moved.

It's another day, another blessing. Thank you, Jesus, glory be to your name, our Lord God reigns. Thanks for the birds that sing as we, also will sing praise unto God.

FEBRUARY 5

Psalm 99:4

The king's strength also loveth judgment thou dost establish equity, thou executest judgment and righteousness in Jacob.

Thank you, Jesus, for strength and waking us up to the land of the living to do all that needed to be done today. We say thank you, Lord.

FEBRUARY 6

Psalm 98:1

O sing unto the LORD a new song; for he hath done marvelous things: his hand, and his holy arm, hath gotten him the victory.

It's a beautiful day. Happy to see a new day. Thank you, Jesus. Make a melody to your God, who is also your creator. Reflecting on those marvelous things He had done.

FEBRUARY 7

1 Thessalonians 5:18

In everything give thanks: for this is the will of God in Christ Jesus concerting you.

Today is a joyful day. Thank you, Jesus, for giving us joy and answering all our prayers. What are your request and petition today? Receive them with thanks. Claim them with praise and worship the Lord.

FEBRUARY 8

Joshua 1:8

This book of the law shall not depart from out of thy mouth; but thou shall meditate therein day and night; that thou mayest observe to do according to all that is written therein: for then thou shalt make thy way prosperous, and then thou shall have good success.

Thank you, Jesus! Great are you, Lord. Your word is powerful, illuminating our lives and giving us success.

FEBRUARY 9

Psalm 100:3

Know ye that the LORD he is God: it is he that hath made us, and not we ourselves; we are his people, and the sheep of his pasture.

Thank you, Lord, for another beautiful day. Your wonders will not cease in our lives, for you made us for your pleasure.

FEBRUARY 10

Acts 1:8

But ye shall receive power, after that the Holy Ghost is come upon you: and ye shall be witnessed unto me both in Jerusalem, and in all Judaea, and in Samaria, and unto the uttermost part of the earth.

Thank you, Jesus. Faithful are you, Lord Almighty. I will continue to praise you. Filling us with your Holy Spirit and Power.

FEBRUARY 11

Psalms 27:1

Wait on the LORD: be of good courage, and he shall strengthen thine heart: wait, I say, on the LORD.

It's a glorious day, hallelujah praise the Lord. Thank you, Jesus, for you're my light and my salvation as I wait upon your promises.

FEBRUARY 12

Psalm 27:1

The LORD is my light and my salvation; whom shall I fear? the LORD is the strength of my life; of whom shall I be afraid?

Hallelujah! Thank you, Jesus. I bless the name of the Lord. My desire would be to dwell in God's house all the days of my life. Amen

FEBRUARY 13

Psalm 34:1

I will bless the LORD at all times: His praise shall continually be in my mouth.

It's another beautiful day. Thank you, Jesus. Your word and praise shall continually be in my mouth.

FEBRUARY 14

John 3:16

For God so loved the world that he gave his only begotten son, that whosoever believeth in him should not perish, but have everlasting life.

Today is Valentine's Day. Thank you, Jesus, for your love for me. Daddy, you love me so much. Give me the grace to love you more and to share your love with others. Amen!

FEBRUARY 15

Proverbs 18:10

The name of the LORD is a strong tower: the righteous runneth into it, and is safe.

Good morning Jesus. Thank you, Jesus. Thanking God for all my people, family, siblings, friends, and brethren for the name of the Lord shall shield us away from every evil.

FEBRUARY 16

Psalm 40:3

And he hath put a new song in my mouth, even praise unto our God: many shall see it, and fear, and shall trust in the LORD.

Praise God, Praise Jesus, Praise the Holy Spirit, Praise the Trinity. God has given me a new song. Hallelujah to His Holy Name. Amen

FEBRUARY 17

Psalm 28:7

The LORD is my strength and my shield; my heart trusted in him, and I am helped: therefore my heart greatly rejoiceth; and with my song will I praise him.

Glory and honor to your Holy Name, Lord. You who made me trust in you, you are my helper, my heart rejoices in your strength, so I will sing a new song.

FEBRUARY 18

Psalm 29:11

The LORD will give strength unto his people; the LORD will bless his people with peace.

Thank you, Jesus. Today is a great day glory be to God Almighty, who gave us peace all around us. Praise Him as He gives strength and peace to His people in which you're one.

FEBRUARY 19

Palms 95:2

Let us come before his presence with thanksgiving, and make a joyful noise unto him with Psalms.

Thank you, Jesus, it's a beautiful day. Glory be to our God. Let us come to His presence with thanksgiving. Praising the Lord.

FEBRUARY 20

Psalms 95:6

O come, let us worship and bow down: let us kneel before the LORD our maker.

Hallelujah! Glory to God, I am saved, I am delivered, and I am healed. Hallelujah, thank you, Lord. Let everything around us come together in ovation to our King.

FEBRUARY 21

Psalm 94:14

For the LORD will not cast off his people, neither will he forsake his inheritance.

It is a new day. Thank you, Jesus, great and marvelous are you, Lord, for not casting us off nor forsaken us.

FEBRUARY 22

Romans 5:1

Therefore being justified by faith we have peace with God through our Lord Jesus Christ.

Thank you, Jesus. Great are you, Lord, for giving us inner peace. I bless your name and will eternally be grateful.

FEBRUARY 23

Isaiah 6:8

Also I heard the voice of the Lord, saying, Whom shall I send and who will go for Us? Then said I, Here am I; send me.

Thank you, Jesus Christ, for meeting the needs of the poor and the homeless as you used me to meet their needs. For you do not work with many but with few. Here am I send me.

FEBRUARY 24

1 John 5:4

For whosoever is born of God overcometh the world: and this is the victory that overcomes the world, even our Faith.

Thank you, Lord. You made us overcome the world. We thank you for our success and victory. We will rejoice and be glad in you.

FEBRUARY 25

2 Chronicles 20:20

And they rose early in the morning... as they went forth, Jehoshaphat stood and said, Hear me....; Believe in the LORD your God, so shall ye be established; believe His Prophets, so shall ye prosper.

Thank you, Jesus. It is a blissful day glory be to God. Believe in your God, and you too shall receive His blessings. Amen.

FEBRUARY 26

2 Chronicles 20:29

And the fear of God was on all the kingdoms of those countries, when they had heard that the LORD fought against the enemies of Israel
(Put your name here.)

Thank you, Jesus. I will continue to thank you all the days of my life in Jesus' name for your faithfulness, fighting for us.

FEBRUARY 27

John 2:1

*And on the third day there was a marriage in Cana
of Galilee and the mother of Jesus was there.*

Thank you, Jesus. Today is my day of
celebration. I will continue to give you praise all
the days of my life. Thank you for being the
center of our marriage. Thank God for your
marriage. If you are still expecting the right
partner, thank God for the bone of your bone, a
friend, not an enemy that God is connecting
you with this year.

FEBRUARY 28

John 11:32; Matthew 8:15

…She fell at His feet…And He touched her hand and the fever left her; and she arose and ministered unto them.

Thank you, Jesus, for it's the last day of the month. Glory be to your name. I will continue to worship you and honor you, for you're worthy to receive all the honor as you hold our hands for healing and for upliftment.

FEBRUARY 29

Revelation 5:12

Saying with a loud voice, Worthy is the Lamb that was slain to receive power, and riches, and wisdom, and strength, and honor, and glory, and blessings.

On Leap Years: Just raise your hands up and continue to praise and worship as the host of heaven is praising Him with their loud voices.

MARCH

The month of March is the month of our moving forward, marching forward, forward ever, and backward never. This month, I and you will march onward and upward In Jesus Name.

MARCH 1

Psalm 119:164

Seven times a day do I praise thee because of thy righteous judgment.

It's a brand new month, a blessed day, and it is my month of elevation. I will do the will of God, by His grace. Thank you, Jesus. Praise the Lord!

MARCH 2

Acts 16:25

And at midnight Paul and Silas prayed, and sang praises unto God: and the prisoners heard them.

Thank you, Jesus, excellent is your name. Glorious are you, giving us victory both during the day and at night. Keep praising the LORD ALMIGHTY, for you don't know who is hearing you for their salvation and deliverance.

MARCH 3

Acts 16:34

And when he had brought them into his house, he set meat before them, and rejoiced believing in God with all his house.

Thank you, Father Lord, for giving us the gift of salvation. Saving us and our household. Thank God for that troublesome husband, wife, child, or siblings and claim the promise of household salvation for them. Your name is praised forever, for we are your people, the elect, and we will continue to praise your name.

MARCH 4

Revelation 19:6

And I heard... saying, Alleluia: for the
Lord God omnipotent reigneth.

Thank you, Jesus, great are you Lord for our
Lord God omnipotent reigns in Jesus name.
Amen.

MARCH 5

Deuteronomy 10:18

He doth execute the judgment of the fatherless and widow, and loveth the stranger, in giving him food and raiment.

Thank you, Jesus. I will continue to praise your name, to give you honor all the days of my life. Taking care of the widows, widowers, orphans, and strangers.

MARCH 6

Psalm 135:1

Praise ye the LORD, Praised ye the name of the LORD. Praise him, O ye servants of the LORD.

Thank you, Jesus, glory be to you, Lord. As your servants, we're praising you, Lord. We say it again Praise ye the name of the Lord. We love your name, and in your name, we have victory.

MARCH 7

Daniel 2:47

The king answered unto Daniel, and said, Of a truth it is, that your God is a God of gods, and Lord of kings, revealer of secrets, seeing thou couldest reveal this secret.

Thank you, Jesus. Awesome and glorious are your names. Thank you for the work of the Holy Spirit in our lives, revealing all secrets to your servants.

MARCH 8

1 Timothy 6:16

Who only hath immortality, dwelling in the light which no man can approach unto, whom no man hath seen, nor can see: to whom be honor and power everlasting. Amen

Thank you, Jesus. Lord, I praise your name. Hallelujah! For you dwell in the light which no man can approach.

MARCH 9

Exodus 14:14

The LORD shall fight for you, and ye shall hold your peace.

Thank you, Jesus. The Lord has fought for His people, and He is still fighting for us. I will give Him all the praise.

MARCH 10

Exodus 15:1

Then sang Moses (put your name) and the children of Israel this song unto the LORD, and spake saying, I will sing unto the LORD, for he hath triumphed gloriously:

Hallelujah! Thank you, Jesus! Glory, glory, I shall continue to praise your name, and I will sing unto the Lord, the song of victory.

MARCH 11

Psalm 8: 1

O LORD, our Lord, how excellent is thy name in all the earth! Who hast set thy glory above the heavens.

It is a beautiful day, and we praise you, Lord. Your glory is up above the heavens. Be thou be glorified.

MARCH 12

Psalm 42:4

... for I had gone with the multitude, I went with them to the house God, with the voice of joy and praise, with a multitude that kept Holy day.

Today is a remarkable day. Thank you, Jesus, for your mighty act in all the nations of the world. Worshipping God with the voice of joy, praise, and gladness.

MARCH 13

Psalm 150:2

Praise him for his mighty acts: praise him according to his excellent greatness.

Thank you, Lord Jesus! You are worthy of my praise. You are the great LORD. I will praise you at all times according to your excellent greatness.

MARCH 14

Psalm 122:6

Pray for the peace of Jerusalem: they shall prosper that love thee.

Thank you, Jesus. Glory be to your name. Hallelujah! As we pray for the peace of Jerusalem, make us prosper according to your word.

MARCH 15

Psalm 90:12

So teach us to number our days, that we may apply our hearts unto wisdom.

I give God the praise and honor, adding another day, another month, and another year to our lives.

MARCH 16

Exodus 23:26

There shall nothing cast their young, nor be barren, in all thy land: the number of thy days I will fulfill.

Thank you, Father God. Thank you, Jesus, and thank you, Holy Spirit. As you all are taking care of the pregnant women. None of them will be barren, their terms shall be completed, and there will be joy in their homes.

.

MARCH 17

1 Peter1:8

Whom having not seen, ye love: in whom, though now ye see him not, yet believing, ye rejoice with joy unspeakable and full of glory.

Praise the Lord. Hallelujah!
You have given us reasons to rejoice, and we are rejoicing.
Thanking you for joy unspeakable.

MARCH 18

Hebrews 10:25

Not forsaking the assembling of ourselves together,
as the manna of some is; ...

Thank you, Jesus, another day, another
blessing. Praise be to your name as we come
together for fellowship with other believers,
both physical, spiritual, and virtual.

MARCH 19

James 4:15

For that ye ought to say, If the Lord will, we shall live, and do this, or that.

Thank you, Jesus. May your name be praised forever. May your will be done in our lives. Our days are planned and ordered by you.

MARCH 20

Psalm 14:6

Ye have shamed the counsel of the poor, because the LORD is his refuge.

Thank you, Jesus. Great is your name, and I worship you. You are my refuge and the counselor of the poor.

MARCH 21

Philippians 2:10

That at the name of Jesus, every knee should bow, of things in heaven, and things in earth, and things under the earth.

Glory be to God hallelujah! Thank you, Jesus, for your faithfulness and kindness at your name all things bow.

MARCH 22

Psalm 147:5

Great is our Lord, and of great power: his understanding is infinite.

You are a great God. I will praise thee all the days of my life in Jesus Christ Mighty Name. Thanking you for the understanding of your word that is the Bible.

MARCH 23

Romans 4:20

He staggered not at the promise of God through unbelief; but was strong in faith, giving glory to God.

Hallelujah! You are awesome, Lord, giving us strong faith amidst our trials, challenges, and odds in life. My life will continue to honor and give you glory in Jesus' name.

MARCH 24

Matthew 28:6

He is not here: for he is risen, as he said. Come, and see the place where the Lord lay.

Who is like unto you Daddy, your name be praised. Hallelujah! Thank you, Jesus, for the power of your resurrection had given us the hope of eternal life.

MARCH 25

Psalm 68:19

Blessed be the Lord, who daily loadeth us with benefits, even the God of our salvation. Selah.

Thank you, Lord Jesus, for daily provisions, benefits, and sustenance. I will continue to thank you.

MARCH 26

Psalm 96:9

O worship the LORD in the beauty of holiness: fear before him, all the earth.

The name of the Lord be praised in all the earth. Thank you, Jesus, for we will worship you in the beauty of your holiness, and we will fear before you.

MARCH 27

Psalm 55:18

He hath delivered my soul in peace from the battle that was against me: for there were many with me.

This is a glorious day. Glory be to God in the highest heaven. Thank you, Jesus Christ, our Lord, for the great deliverance given to us.

MARCH 28

Psalm 135:20

Bless the LORD, O house of Levi: Ye that fear the LORD, bless the LORD.

Worthy are you, oh Lord, and you are worthy to be honored. Because I fear you, I will continue to bless you and say thank you.

MARCH 29

1 Chronicles 16:34

O give thanks unto the LORD; for he is good; for his mercy endureth forever

You are to be praised, and I say thank you, Jesus, for you have been good to us in all our ways.

MARCH 30

Colossians 3:15

And let the peace of God rule in your hearts, to the which also ye are called in one body; and be ye thankful.

Wonderful and excellent are you, Lord, for your compassion towards me. I am thankful to you, Jesus.

MARCH 31

Colossians 4:2

Continue in prayer, and watch in the same with thanksgiving.

The Lord had made us march forward, and so we are. So are you too. Keep marching forward for the rest of your life, and give thanks.

APRIL

John 11:25

Jesus said unto her, I am the resurrection, and the life: he that believeth in me, though he were dead, yet shall he live.

It is our month of resurrection. Every dead thing in our lives will resurrect in Jesus Christ Mighty Name. Amen. Thank you, Lord.

APRIL 1

Matthew 28: 17

And when they saw him, they worshipped him: but some doubted.

Thank you for making us see another new month. Your name is to be Praised and be Worshipped. "Truly it's our day, week, month and season of celebration and joy "in Jesus Mighty Name. Amen!

APRIL 2

Luke 24:36

And as they thus spake, Jesus himself stood in the midst of them, and said unto them, Peace be unto you.

Thank you, Jesus, for faithful is your name. I praise the name of the Lord, and I will continue to honor His name for His peace that abides with us.

APRIL 3

Revelation 4:10

The four and twenty elders fall down before him that sat on the throne, and worship him that liveth for ever and ever, and cast their crowns before the throne, saying.

Today is a day of worship, praise, and adoration to the Lord our King. Bow before His throne and worship Him.

APRIL 4

Psalm 103:1-2

Bless the LORD O my soul: and all that is within me, bless his holy name. Bless the LORD O my soul: and forget not all his benefits.

Bless the Lord, O my soul. Let all that is in me bless His holy name. He had been so good to us. Please forget not all his good wills toward you. Let everyone give Him praise now and always.

APRIL 5

Luke 1:46

And Mary said, My soul doth magnify the Lord.

My soul magnifies the Lord and lets His name be praised. Amen. It is a blessing seeing our children growing physically and spiritually.

APRIL 6

Psalm 18:49

Therefore will I give thanks unto thee, O Lord, among the heathen, and sing praises unto thy name.

Hallelujah! I will exalt the Lord, and His praise shall continually be in my mouth. Let us all give Him praise from the bottom of our hearts.

APRIL 7

Psalm 134:2

Lift up your hands in the sanctuary and bless the LORD.

We all will come to the house of the Lord and lift up our hands to give Him praise. Wherever you find yourself today, either online, in-person, via Zoom, YouTube, Facebook, or on any social media platforms, lift your voice and your hands up and praise the Lord.

APRIL 8

Romans 8:31

What shall we then say to these things? If God be for us, who can be against us?

Worthy is your name, oh Lord, and I will exalt you now and forever. For as long as you are with me, Lord, no one can be against me.

APRIL 9

Luke 18:19

And Jesus said unto him, why callest thou me good?
None is good, Save one, that is, God.

Praise the Lord! Praise the Lord! Hallelujah!
Hallelujah! For God is good to me, making His
sun shines on us and His rain on us. Our God is
good to us always.

APRIL 10

Psalm 48:1

Great is the LORD, and greatly to be praised in the city of our God, in the mountain of his holiness.

Thank you, Jesus. Great is your name, and you are great to be praised. You are the greatest of all—we worship You.

APRIL 11

Acts 5:19 - 20

But the Angel of the Lord by night opened the prison doors, and brought them forth, and said, Go, stand and speak in the temple to the people all the words of this life.

The everlasting Father, we thank you, and we praise you for you are the one who sees and knows everything. You opened the prison doors and liberated your own. Nothing is too difficult for you to do.

APRIL 12

Psalm 48:14

For this God is our God for ever and ever: he will be our guide even unto death.

Thank you, Lord, for you are our God. You will guide and protect us from now even unto death.

APRIL 13

Job 33:12

Behold, in this thou art not just: I will answer thee, that God is greater than

man.

Thank you, Jesus Christ. You are God in man but greater than man. Blessed be to your name.

APRIL 14

Psalm 18:31

For who is God, save the Lord? or who is a Rock save our God?

Thank you, Jesus Christ. You are our Lord and Rock. We will not cease to praise you, and we will not relent.

APRIL 15

Micah 7:18

Who is a God like unto thee that pardoneth iniquity, and passeth by the transgressions of the remnant of his heritage? He retaineth not his anger forever, because he delighteth in mercy.

Praise the Lord most high. Hear what Prophet Micah penned in his book, saying God is the one that pardoned our sins and iniquities.

APRIL 16

Mark 12:32

And the Scribe said unto him, Well, Master, thou hast said the truth: for there is one God; and there is none other but he:

There is only one God and none other. Blessed be His Holy Name. Do you believe that? Give Him praise, worship Him and Adore Him.

APRIL 17

Romans 8:35

Who shall separate us from the love of Christ? Shall tribulation, or distress, or persecution, or famine, or nakedness, or peril, or sword?

Thank you, Father God, for if you are with us, no one can be against us, and nothing shall separate us from you.

APRIL 18

Romans 15:13

Now the God of hope fill you with all joy and peace in believing, that ye may abound in hope, through the power of the Holy Spirit.

Thank you, our Lord Jesus, the God of our hope, as you fill us with all joy today and always.

APRIL 19

1 Corinthians 15:28b

...that God may be all in all.

Oh God of our lives, you are the all in all, we love you, Father God. We thank you for being our father and for being overall.

APRIL 20

2 Corinthians 1:3

Blessed be God, even the Father of our Lord Jesus Christ, and Father of mercies, and the God of all comfort.

Thank you, Jesus, for you are the God of mercies and also the God of all comforts that comfort us during the time of sorrow and bereavement.

APRIL 21

1 John 5:20

...that we may know him that is true, and we are in him that is true, even his son Jesus Christ. This is the true God and eternal life.

We thank you, the true and Triune God, for making us to know you. May your name be praised forever.

APRIL 22

Genesis 43:29

...And he said, God be gracious unto thee, my son.

Thank you, Jesus Christ, for being merciful and gracious to us in all our ways. You did not count our sins and iniquities against us but loved us. We love you in return.

APRIL 23

Nehemiah 9:31

Nevertheless for thy great mercies' sake thou didst not utterly consume them, nor forsake them: for thou art a gracious and merciful God.

Thank you, Jesus Christ, for your unfailing love and compassion for not forsaking us and being gracious to us.

APRIL 24

Psalm 86:15

But thou, O Lord, art a God full of compassion, and gracious, long suffering and plenteous in mercy and truth.

Our God, full of compassion and grace, we bow down before your throne. Hallow be to your Holy Name.

APRIL 25

1 Peter 2:3

If so be ye have tasted that the Lord is gracious.

Yes Lord, thank you for I have tasted of you.
You are good and gracious to my taste.

APRIL 26

Joel 2:13

And rend your heart, and not your garments, and turn unto the LORD your God: for he is gracious and merciful, slow to anger, and of great kindness, and repenteth him of the evil.

Thank you, Jesus. I will praise you daily according to your command. I give thanks for you are gracious and merciful.

APRIL 27

Deuteronomy 4:35

Unto thee it was shewed, that thou mightest know that the LORD he is God; there is none else beside him.

Today and every tomorrow, you are God, the Savior, the healer, and all in all. Glory be unto you, Lord.

APRIL 28

1 Samuel 2:1

And Hannah prayed, and said, My heart rejoiceth in the LORD, ...

My heart rejoices in you, oh Lord, for no one else like you. Keep rejoicing all is well.

APRIL 29

Proverbs 3:5

Trust in the Lord with all thy heart and lean not unto your own understanding.

Thank you, Jesus, for helping me trust in you for all daily needs, decisions made, and daily choices.

APRIL 30

Isaiah 37:20

Now therefore, O LORD our God, save us from his hand, that all the kingdom of the earth may know that thou art the LORD, even thou only.

Thank you, oh Lord our God, for saving us from all our enemies and glorifying yourself in our lives. Blessed be thy name.

Thank you, Jesus, for who you are and for always being there for me to see me through the month as I am looking forward to a victorious new month.

MAY

May is our month of ceaseless blessings, double and triple blessings. Mother's Day, birthdays, and graduation month.

MAY 1

2 Chronicles 5:13

...to make one sound to be heard in praising and thanking the LORD... then the house was filled with cloud, even the house of the LORD.

Thank you, Jesus Christ. As we enter into this great month of triple blessings. May your name continuously be praised. May our lives and our homes be filled with your presence.

MAY 2

Deuteronomy 10:21

He is thy praise, and he is thy God, that hath done for thee these great and terrible things, which thy eyes have seen.

Praise the Lord, for you are my praise. You are my God. Indeed your hands had performed these great and terrible things that we have seen around us. All glory be to your Name.

MAY 3

Judges 5:2

Praise ye the LORD for the avenger of Israel, when the people willingly offered themselves.

I will sing praise to the Lord God, for you have been good to me. I will willingly offer the sacrifice of praise and thanks.

MAY 4

2 Samuel 22: 4

I will call on the LORD, who is worthy to be praised:
so shall I be saved from mine enemies.

There is none worthy of being praised, except
you, Lord. Calling upon your name is a
blessing. Thank you, Lord Jesus.

MAY 5

Psalm 7:17

I will praise the Lord according to his faithfulness: and will sing praise to the name of the LORD most high.

Thank you, Lord, take all the praise and worship, for none is like you in all the earth. Thank you, Jesus.

MAY 6

Psalm 9:1

I will praise thee, O LORD, with my whole heart; I will shew forth all thy marvelous works.

I will praise thee, my Lord, with all that is in me, out of me, around me, and I will show forth all thy marvelous works to all and sundry.

MAY 7

Psalm 22:25

My praise shall be of thee in the great congregation: I will pay my vows before them that fear him.

Thank you, Jesus, for the fear and love of God in me. You are my testimony — I will praise you amid a living congregation.

MAY 8

Psalm 30:9

What profit is there in my blood when I go down to the pit? Shall the dust praise thee? Shall it declare thy truth?

Shall the dust praise thee? No Lord, the living will praise you, and I will praise you. Because you that is reading this devotional is alive, praise him the more.

MAY 9

Psalm 65:1

Praise waiteth for thee, O God, in Sion: and unto thee shall the vow be performed.

My praise waiteth for you, O God. Receive the glory as I pay my vow of praise.

MAY 10

1 Thessalonians 5:16

Rejoice evermore.

Thanking God for answering our prayers, request, and petitions.

The name of the Lord is exalted, for making us rejoice over our children, children's children even unto the fourth generation. Thank you, Jesus.

MAY 11

Psalm 100:2

Make a joyful noise unto the LORD, all ye lands.

Thank you, Jesus, wonderful is your name,
great is your name, excellent is your name,
majesty is your name as we make a joyful noise
to you, Lord.

MAY 12

John 8:58

Jesus said unto them, Verily, verily, I say unto you,
Before Abraham was, I am.

Hallelujah, glory, worthy are you O God and greatly to be praised. It is a great day which the Lord has made. Let us rejoice in it. The God of our fathers for Jesus said before Abraham was, I am.

MAY 13

Revelation 19:1

And after these things, I heard a great voice of much people in heaven, saying, Alleluia; Salvation, and glory, and honor, and power, unto the Lord our God.

Shout a big ALLELUIA our God reigns. Thank you, Jesus, for reigning in our lives. We are for you all our days. Amen

MAY 14

Revelation 19:6

And I heard as it was the voice of a great multitude, and as the voice of many waters, and as the voice of Mighty thundering, saying, Alleluia; for the Lord God omnipotent reigneth.

The Lord God omnipotent reigns. Thank you, Jesus—you reign forever.

MAY 15

Psalm 96:4

For the LORD is great, and greatly to be praised: he is to be feared above all gods.

The Lord is good, great, and greatly to be praised. We give you all the glory.

~ GIVE THANKS ALL THE YEAR ROUND ~

MAY 16

Psalm 63:3

*Because thy loving kindness is better than life, my
lips shall praise thee.*

Thank you, Jesus. My lips shall praise you
forever. Why? Because your lovingkindness is
better than life.

MAY 17

Psalm 65:1

Praise waiteth for thee, O God, in Sion: and unto thee shall the vow be performed.

Thank you, Jesus, praise waited for thee O God. Today lavish God with your praise. He will do the impossible in your life.

MAY 18

Psalm 88:10

Wilt thou shew wonders to the dead? Shall the dead arise and praise thee? Selah.

Every day I will praise thee. I will give thee thanks for this is the command. I will continue to praise your name for the dead will not praise thee.

MAY 19

Genesis 2:7

And the LORD God formed man of the dust of ground, and breathed into his nostrils the breath of life; and man became a living soul.

Many times a day, with each breath that I take, will I praise you the rock of my salvation and the breath of my life.

MAY 20

Psalm 100:5

For the LORD is good; his mercy is everlasting: and his truth endureth to all generations.

Praise the Lord! My God, You are good. Seeing the beauty of this new day for your mercy is everlasting.

MAY 21

Psalm 106:1

Praise ye the LORD, O give thanks unto the LORD; for he is good for his mercy endureth for ever.

Thank you, Jesus. O give thanks unto the LORD for all and for everything. Our Lord Jesus is good, and indeed His mercy is forever.

May 22

Psalm 119:89

For ever, O LORD, thy word is settled in heaven.

Forever Lord almighty, Your word is settled in the highest heaven, and therefore will I give you thanks.

MAY 23

Matthew 1:21

And she shall bring forth a son, and thou shall call his Name JESUS: for he shall save his people from their sins.

I am praising you, Lord, from the bottom of my heart because you have done so much for me. My Lord and Savior.

MAY 24

Isaiah 38:19

The living, the living, he shall praise thee, as I do this day: the father to the children shall make known thy truth. Thank you, Lord!

Eternal God, You are God of the living. The living shall praise and worship you, Lord. Thank you, Jesus Christ, for I am a living being.

MAY 25

Philippians 2:11

And that every tongue should confess that Jesus Christ is Lord, to the glory of God the father.

If the hairs of my head turned to tongues, not enough to praise, worship, and thank you. But with the one and only tongue given to me, I will continually use it to say, "thank you, Father, thank you Son, and thank you Holy Spirit."

MAY 26

Isaiah 9:6

For unto us a child is born, unto us a son is given: and the government shall be upon his shoulder: and his name shall be called Wonderful, Counsellor, The Mighty God, The everlasting Father, The Prince of Peace.

Ha! Wow! How wonderful and gracious are you, Lord, beyond comprehension. Thank you for your unfailing love.

MAY 27

Isaiah 9:7

Of the increase of His government and peace, there shall be no end, upon the throne of David, and upon his kingdom, to order it, and to establish with judgment and with justice from henceforth even forever. The zeal of the LORD of hosts will perform this.

Have not seen an awesome God like you doing great and marvelous things in the life of all your creatures. The beautiful and colorful God. There is an abundance of peace in your government. Praise the Lord! Hallelujah!

MAY 28

Psalm 8:4

*What is man, that thou art mindful of him? and the
son of man, that thou visitest him?*

Who is man Lord, that you take cognizance of
him, the dust of the earth, this amazes me, so I
say thank you in trillion times trillion times.

MAY 29

1 Samuel 2:2

There is none holy as the LORD: for there is none beside thee: neither is there any rock like our God.

As we are getting closer to the end of the month, I look back and say a big THANK YOU JESUS. No one like you, neither is there any rock of defense like our God.

MAY 30

1 Thessalonians 5:19

Quench not the the Spirit.

Thanking you, Lord, for vision and revelation through your Spirit that keeps me going spiritually.

MAY 31

Acts 3:8

And he leaping up stood, and walked, and entered with them into the temple, walking, and leaping, and praising God.

It is the last day of the month. Praise ye the LORD! We shall stand up, walk, enter into the temple of our God—praising Jehovah. Thank you, Lord Jesus. Blessed be your holy name for all your blessings upon your children and the Church. For losing our bonds, for breaking our yokes, and for liberating us.

JUNE

It is the half of the year. We are very grateful to You, our Most High God, for being there for us and sustaining us. Glory, Hallelujah!

JUNE 1

Psalm 104:1

Bless the LORD, O my soul. O LORD my God, thou art very great; thou art clothed with honor and majesty.

My soul blessed the Lord for a new month. The month of greater glory and elevation. Thank you, Jesus, for you are clothed in majesty and glory.

JUNE 2

1 Timothy 6:16

Who only hath immortality, dwelling in the light which no man can approach unto; whom no man hath seen, nor can see: to whom be honor and power everlasting. Amen

It is another season of blessings and celebration as we continue honoring our God almighty. He will, in return, bless us.

JUNE 3

2 Thessalonians 2:13

*But we are bound to give thanks always to God
...because God hath from the beginning chosen you
to salvation through sanctification of the spirit and
belief of the truth.*

Today, tomorrow, and all days will I give Him
thanks for all the Lord has done. You have
chosen us for salvation through sanctification of
the spirit, and our faith is in you.

JUNE 4

Deuteronomy 32:4

He is the Rock, his work is perfect: for all his ways are judgment: a God of truth and without iniquity, just and right is he.

The Lord had done so much for me. I cannot tell it all, neither can I thank Him enough. He is perfect in all He ways.

JUNE 5

2 Chronicles 2:5

And the house which I build is great: for great is our God above all gods.

Great is the Lord, doing wonderful things in the lives of His children. Our body is your temple and your dwelling place. And we shall not misuse our body. Thank you, Jesus, for making our body your abode.

JUNE 6

Job 37:23

Touching the Almighty we can not find Him out: he is excellent in power, and in judgment, and in plenty of justices: he will not afflict.

Excellent is our God, excellent in power doing excellent work. Glory and adoration be unto our Lord. Your Excellency O LORD!

JUNE 7

Psalm 127:1

Except the Lord build the house, they labor in vain that build it: except the LORD keep the city, the watchman waketh but in vain.

Wonderful is our God showing His wonderful love to mankind doing wonderful things, for we are created by Him wonderfully. Thank you, Lord, for those protecting us, the watchmen, the servicemen and women of the military, the marines, and all the law enforcement officers. We bless you for watching over them and their families.

JUNE 8

Psalm 31:19

Oh how great is thy goodness, which thou hast laid up for them that fear thee: which thou hast wrought for them that trust thee before the sons of men!

How great is our God, sing with me. How great is our God! He is greater than the greatest. Thank you, Jesus.

JUNE 9

Isaiah 40:28

Hast thou not known? Hast thou not heard? That the everlasting God, the Lord, the creator of the ends of the earth, fainteth not, neither is weary? There's no searching of his understanding.

We give you praise, and we say thank you, Lord. You faint not, nor are you weary. No one can search for your understanding.

JUNE 10

Psalm 5:12

For thou, LORD, will bless the righteous; with Favour will thou compass him as with a shield.

Thank you, Jesus. You are our shield. The only wise God who favors us in all areas of our lives. Today as we step out, doors of favor will open for our sake.

JUNE 11

Lamentation 3:22-23

It is the LORD'S mercies that we are not consumed, because his compassions fail not. They are new every morning: great is thy faithfulness.

Thank you, Lord Jesus, for waking me up to a brighter morning and into the land of the living. Great is your faithfulness.

JUNE 12

2 Chronicles 20:15

...thus saith the Lord unto you, be not afraid nor dismayed by reason of this great multitude: for the battle is not yours, but God's.

Thank you, Jesus Christ--the mighty man in battle, fighting all my battles. I shall not be afraid nor be dismayed. You are my God.

JUNE 13

1 John 4:4

Ye are of God little children, and have overcome them: because greater is he that is in you, than he that is in the world.

Thank you, Jesus Christ, Holy Spirit, for living in me and showing your Mighty works in the life of all Christians.

JUNE 14

James 1:27

Pure religion and undefiled before God and the father is this, to visit the fatherless and widows in their affliction, and to keep himself unspotted from the world.

Thank you, Jesus Christ, son of the most high God, for taking care of the poor, the needy, the afflicted, the oppressed, and those who are mourning, giving them comfort.

JUNE 15

Hosea 14:3

...for in thee the fatherless findeth mercy.

Father God, we praise you for caring for the orphans, widows, and widowers, showing them your mercy. You are the father of the fatherless.

JUNE 16

1 Timothy 2:1-2

I exhort therefore, that first of all, supplications prayers, intercessions, and giving of thanks be made for all men; for kings and for all that are in authority; that we may lead a quiet and peaceable life in all godliness and honesty.

Holy Spirit, thank you for your anointing over all ministers of God: Pastors, General Overseers, Presidents, Founders, Inventors, and for all that are in authority. Help us to lead a quiet and peaceful life in all godliness and honesty. Praise be to your holy name.

JUNE 17

Matthew 21:22

*And all things, whatsoever ye shall ask in prayer,
believing, ye shall receive.*

Thank you, Jesus, for showing up for us. For the
demonstration of your power in the lives of
your children and answering our prayers
always.

JUNE 18

John 1:1

In the beginning was the Word, and the Word was with God, and Word was God.

Thank you, Lord, for giving us your words, the Bible, and all the promises you have promised us.

JUNE 19

Revelation 1:8

I am Al'-pha and O-me'-ga, the beginning and the ending, saith the Lord, which is, and which was, and which is to come, the Almighty.

Thank you, Jesus Christ. You are our Alpha and Omega. Our beginning and our ending, unto you we are all coming. Praise the Lord!

JUNE 20

Psalm 121:1-2

I will lift up my eyes unto the hill, from whence cometh my help, My help cometh from the LORD, which made heaven and earth.

Thank you, Jesus Christ, for sending help from above and not from abroad.
Our present helps in times of trouble.

JUNE 21

Isaiah 6:3

And one cried unto another, and said, Holy, Holy, Holy is the LORD of host: the whole earth is full of his glory.

A beautiful day indeed. Glory be to your holy name Lord. The whole earth is full of your glory, and from one end to the other, we will say Holy, Holy, Holy, is the LORD of Host.

JUNE 22

James 1:17

Every good gifts, and every perfect gift is from above, and cometh down from the Father of lights, with whom is no variableness, neither shadow of turning.

Father of light, we bless you for all the things you have made us known through the Holy Spirit, for the gifts, and for the fruit of the Holy Spirit. Thank you.

JUNE 23

1 Timothy 2:5

For there is one God, and one mediator between God and men, the man Christ Jesus.

We give thanks, Jesus Christ our mediator, interceding for us always. Do you know that somebody somewhere is praying for you? Give thanks and praise to God on behalf of someone today.

JUNE 24

Proverbs 25:25

As cold water to a thirsty soul, so is good news from a far country.

Jesus Christ, we thank you for good news from far and near that gladdens our hearts. You made us be the carrier of the good news of the gospel. This we shall continue to do.

JUNE 25

Psalm 68:19

Blessed be the Lord, who daily loadeth us with benefits, even the God of our salvation.

We say thank you, Lord Jesus, for all the provisions and generosity given to us in your name. They are all undeniable.

JUNE 26

Numbers 14:19

Pardon, I beseech thee, the iniquity of this people according unto the greatness of thy mercy, and as thou hast forgiven this people, from Egypt even until now.

Thank you, Father God, for not counting our iniquities against us and for showing us your mercy. We are your people. We love you, Father.

JUNE 27

Hebrews 13:8

Jesus Christ the same yesterday, and today and forever.

Jesus Christ, we thank you for yesterday, today, and tomorrow. You remain the same. You never change, but you change worst situations to good, good to better, and better to best. That is who you are.

JUNE 28

Romans 8:1

There is therefore now no condemnation to them which are in Christ Jesus, who walk not after the flesh, but after the Spirit.

Thank you, Jesus Christ, our Savior, Redeemer, Justifier, and Coming King for not condemning us. We will not walk after the flesh, but we will be filled with your Spirit.

JUNE 29

Romans 15:13

Now the God of hope fill you with all joy and peace in believing, that ye may abound in hope, through the power of the Holy Ghost.

Thank you, Jesus Christ. You are the only hope of the world. You are my hope, no one else. Do you hope in God? If yes, give Him praise for whoever hopes in Him will never be confused, confounded, depressed, or hopeless.

JUNE 30

John 1:5

And the light shineth in darkness; and the darkness comprehended it not.

Thank you, Jesus Christ, father of light, for giving us your unquenchable light.

Last day of the month, praise and adoration be unto our God for safety and divine protection all these days, weeks, and months. Hallelujah!

205

JULY

July is our month of freedom.

Thanking God for both Physical, Financial, and especially Spiritual freedom. Hallelujah!

JULY 1

Psalm 4:5

Offer the sacrifices of righteousness and put your trust in the LORD.

We shall offer to our God the sacrifices of righteousness in our land, and we will continually put our trust in the LORD.

JULY 2

Psalm 71:5

For thou art my hope, O LORD GOD, thou art my trust from my youth.

Thank you, Lord Jesus Christ, we have put our trust in You right from our youth, Oh Lord of grace. We will continue to trust in You.

JULY 3

Job 13:15

Though he slay me, yet will I trust in him: but I will maintain mine own ways before him.

Thank you, Father God--our trust is in you. We will maintain our ways before You. Our nations will love You. Our country will be obedient to your commandments and status, and we will all trust in You.

JULY 4

Psalm 125:1

They that trust in the LORD shall be as mount Zion, which cannot be removed, but abideth forever.

Happy 4th of July. Thank you, Jesus, for total freedom. Freedom from Slavery. Freedom from sin, flesh, attack of the enemies, and also from prayerlessness — and for abiding with us forever.

JULY 5

Acts 2:1

And when the day of Pentecost was fully come, they were all with one accord in one place.

Thank you, Jesus Christ, for helping us have sweet fellowship with the Father, Son, and Holy Spirit, making all believers in Christ be in one accord, in one place, and in you. Praise the Lord!

JULY 6

1 Corinthians 15:58

Therefore my beloved brethren, be ye steadfast, unmovable, always abounding in the work of the Lord, forasmuch as ye know that your labor is not in vain in the Lord.

The name of the Lord be praised for our labor in your vineyard is not in vain. We shall be steadfast till we see you in glory. We will not be moved — we will continue to abide in the work of our God.

JULY 7

Acts 2:4

And they were all filled with the Holy Ghost, and began to speak with other tongues, as the Spirit gave them utterance.

Holy Spirit, the third in the Trinity, thank you for giving us the utterances to speak in diverse languages and in tongues. Awesome and excellent, are you in the midst of your people.

JULY 8

Psalm 9:10

And they that know your name will put their trust in thee: for thou LORD, hast not forsaken them that seek thee.

Because we know your name, that is why we put our trust in you. Thank you, Jesus. You will not forsake us.

JULY 9

Psalm 22:22

I will declare thy name unto my brethren: in the midst of the congregation will I praise thee.

We shall declare your name among the brethren, and we shall praise you forever amid the congregation.

JULY 10

Isaiah 26:4

Trust ye in the LORD for ever: for in the LORD JEHOVAH is everlasting strength:

Our Lord, we praise you for our trust is in you. Thank you for helping us to trust in you. You are our everlasting strength.

JULY 11

Exodus 15:11

Who is like unto thee, O LORD, among the gods?
Who is like thee, glorious in holiness, fearful in
praises, doing wonders?

Thank you, Jesus, for our God is glorious in
holiness and fearful in praise.
We trust in you. Amen

JULY 12

Psalm 22:3

But thou art Holy, O thou that inhabitest the praises of Israel.

Glory be to the Lord in the highest, for he inhabits the praise of His people. Praise Him from the bottom of your heart.

JULY 13

Luke 2:13

*And suddenly there was with the Angel a multitude
of the heavenly host praising God...*

Hallelujah, our Lord God Jehovah Shalom
reigns. The angels and the multitude of the
heavenly host are praising you, Lord. One of
these days to come, we shall join the heavenly
hosts in giving you thanks none stop.

JULY 14

Psalm 149:6

Let the high praises of God be in their mouth, and a two edged sword in their hand:

Let your high praise continue to be in our mouths. Lord of heaven, we praise you. You are always at our side.

JULY 15

Psalm 78:4

We will not hide them from their children, shewing to the generation to come the praises of the LORD, and his strength, and his wonderful works that he hath done.

My Jehovah Jire, the great provider, I cannot thank you enough. Today is a great day in my life. Thank you for the air, water, and all essentials of life you have provided us with. Our unborn generation will continue to declare your praise. Thank you, Jesus Christ.

JULY 16

Philippians 3:4

…If any other man thinketh that he hath whereof he might trust in the flesh, I more.

Thank you, Jesus, for we do not trust in our flesh, but we trust in your Holy Name. Blessed be your Name forever.

JULY 17

Nehemiah 1:5

And said, I beseech thee, O LORD God of heaven, the great and terrible God, that keepeth covenant and mercy for them that love him and observe his commandments:.

God had done great and terrible things which our eyes have seen. Thank you, Jesus, for your love, compassion, and mercies that are new every morning.

JULY 18

Mark 10:24

… Children, how hard is it for them that trust in riches to enter into the kingdom of God!

O Lord our God, we do not trust in our riches, but we trust in you alone to live a quiet, peaceful life and to enter the kingdom of God.

JULY 19

Psalm 33:8

*Let all the earth fear the LORD: let all the
inhabitants of the world stand in awe of Him.*

Thank you, Jesus. It is a command from the
Lord. I will pay my vow to you, for you are
wonderful and excellent in all your ways.

JULY 20

John 14:26

But the comforter, which is the Holy Ghost, whom the Father will send in my name, he shall teach you all things, and bring all things to your remembrance, whatsoever I have said unto you.

Thank you, Jesus Christ, for giving us the Holy Spirit to dwell in us and continue to direct us and remind us of the Father's love.

JULY 21

Songs of Solomon 2:4

He brought me to the banqueting house, and his banner over me was love.

Jehovah God, thanks be to you, Lord, for your unfailing love lavished on us and also for your banner of love.

JULY 22

Romans 15:13

Now the God of hope fill you with all joy and peace in believing, that ye may abound in hope, through the power of the Holy Ghost.

Thank you, Jesus Christ, for another beautiful day and for your love to mankind, for hope and power. Glory be unto your name.

JULY 23

2 Kings 4:26

Run now, I pray thee, to meet her, and say unto her, is it well with thee? Is it well with thy husband? Is it well with the child? And she answered, It is well.

Today as I heard His voice, it is well with me, my husband, children, jobs, and everything that concerns me. Thank you, Jesus.

JULY 24

Deuteronomy 15:11; Matthew 26:11

For the poor shall never cease out of the land: therefore I command thee, saying, Thou shall open thine hand wide unto thy brother, to thy poor, and to thy needy, in thy land. For ye have the poor always with you; but me ye have not always.

Thank you, Jesus, for the poor among us, for providing food for them and meeting their needs. We shall always have you with us. Praise be to your name.

JULY 25

John 6:37

All that the father giveth me shall come to me: and him that cometh to me I will in no wise cast out.

Thank you, Jesus, for free salvation given to us for whosoever come unto you, you will not cast away. We praise you for this love.

JULY 26

Matthew 6:10

Thy kingdom come. Thy will be done in earth as it is done in heaven.

Thank you, Jesus, for giving the leaders (both spiritual and political) directions to rule the world according to your will, with your power and wisdom.

JULY 27

1Timothy 5:3; Lamentation 5:3

Honor widows that are widows in deed. We are orphans and fatherless, our mothers are as widows.

Thank you, our Father in heaven, for taking care of the refugees, the immigrants, and those who lost their loved ones due to wars and disasters due to the pandemic, epidemic, collapsed building, mass shooting, etc. Lord, you own and love them. We thank you!

JULY 28

Exodus 1:17

But the midwives feared God, and did not as the king of Egypt commanded them, but saved the men children alive.

Thank you, Jesus Christ, for taking care of the pregnant women, their pregnancy, and their babies. Thank you for fear of God upon our doctors and nurses. Praise be unto your Holy Name.

JULY 29

Psalm 85:6

Wilt thou not revive us again: that thy people may rejoice in thee?

Thank you, Jesus Christ, for reviving the Church and recruiting sinners to become saints. Glory be unto your name.

JULY 30

Luke 18:1.

And he spake a parable unto them to this end, that men ought always to pray, and not to faint.

Thank you, Jesus Christ, for helping us be mindful of prayers and the power of prayer you have put in us. Praise and honor be unto you. Amen.

JULY 31

Proverbs 18:10

The name of the LORD is a strong tower: the righteous runneth into it, and is safe.

Today is the last day of the month. Thank you, Jesus Christ, for your divine protection over our lives. We give you praise for making us see the end of July. Glory be to your name.

~ GIVE THANKS ALL THE YEAR ROUND ~

AUGUST

Thank you, Lord, for our students are on
vacation during this month. You will keep them
safe from all evil occurrences. Amen

AUGUST 1

1 Kings 6:38

And in the eleventh year, in the month Bul, which is the eighth month, was the house finished throughout all the parts thereof, and according to all the fashion of it...

It is a new month. Thank you for you will see us through this new month. Good news shall be our portion in Jesus Mighty Name. All the good things God has started will come to fulfillment in our lives in Jesus Mighty Name Amen.

AUGUST 2

Exodus 4:11

And the LORD said unto him, Who hath made man's mouth? or who maketh the dumb, or deaf, or the seeing, or the blind? have not I the LORD?

Thank you, Jesus, for making us see another day. Thank you for taking care of the disabled. They are yours, Lord. We praise you.

AUGUST 3

Daniel 12:4

...many shall run to and fro, and knowledge shall be increased.

Thank you, Jesus, for giving us geniuses around the world who are specialized in all areas such as science, medical, education, business, technology, marketing, politics, and all religious founders whom you called for your own glory.

AUGUST 4

Psalm 145:1

I will extol thee, my God, O king; and I will bless thy name for ever and ever.

Thank you, Jesus, for you are mighty and great. I will exalt your name Lord from now till eternity.

AUGUST 5

Luke 15:7

I say unto you, that likewise joy shall be in heaven over one sinner that repenteth, more than over ninety and nine just persons, which need no repentance.

Thank you, Father God, for I cannot but praise you for helping me repent from my sins, for the forgiveness I received, and for joy in heaven over sinners who repent.

AUGUST 6

John 14:18

I will not leave you comfortless: I will come to you.

Thank you, Holy Spirit, for comforting and encouraging us daily. You will abide with us, and we shall abide in you. We accept you into our lives by faith.

AUGUST 7

John 14:16

*And I will pray the Father, and he shall give you
another Comforter, that he may abide with you
forever:*

Thank you, Holy Spirit, for performing signs
and wonders during our days and abiding with
us forever. Truly these signs shall follow them
that believes says the Lord Jesus Christ.

AUGUST 8

John 15:26

But when the Comforter is come, whom I will send unto from the Father, even the Spirit of truth, which proceedeth from the Father, he shall testify of me:

Holy Spirit, we thank you for helping all our leaders do the right things, do God's will, and preach the truth of your word. We shall testify of you to the world.

AUGUST 9

Luke 9:43

And they were all amazed at the mighty power of God...

Thank you, Father God, you amazed all the people around me when they saw your mighty power moving in my life. As you read this devotional, His word will be fulfilled in your life, and His wonders will amaze people around you. Give Him praise.

AUGUST 10

Isaiah 1:19

If ye be willing and obedient, ye shall eat the good of the land.

Thank you, Father God, for creating the heavens and the earth and making us eat the good of the land as we obey you.

AUGUST 11

Genesis 1:28

And God bless them, and God said unto them, be fruitful and multiply, and replenish the earth, and subdue it: and have dominion over the fish of the sea, and over the fowl of the air, and over every living thing that moveth upon the earth.

Thank you, Father God, Jesus Christ, for creating human beings to have dominion over your world and all you have made.

AUGUST 12

Genesis 1:31

And God saw every thing he had made, and, behold, it was very good. And the evening and the morning were the sixth day.

Thank you, Father God, for you created our world in six days with all the beautiful things in different colors. God, you are so colorful!

AUGUST 13

Genesis 1:26

And God said, Let us make man in our image, after our likeness...

Father God, we thank you. With your Son and your Spirit, you created man and woman in your own image. We love and cherish how you made us. My image is God's image. I will not change it to something else. This image of me will continue to honor God.

AUGUST 14

Psalm 115:11

Ye that fear the LORD, trust in the LORD: he is their help and their shield.

We fear you, O LORD our GOD. We trust in you. Thank you for being our helper and our shield. Help us to trust in you more.

AUGUST 15

Psalm 118:24

This is the day which the Lord hath made; we will rejoice and be glad in it.

This is the day the Lord has made we will rejoice, be glad, be happy, and be filled with praise. Thank you, Jesus, for you are our joy.

AUGUST 16

1 Corinthians 1:24

But unto them which are called, both Jews and Greeks, Christ the power of God, and the wisdom of God.

Thank you, Jesus Christ, you are the wisdom of God, who has given man all wisdom to invent, produce, examine, find out all those things that we benefited from today.

AUGUST 17

Revelation 21:1

And I saw a new heaven and a new earth: for the first heaven and the first earth were passed away; and there was no more sea.

Thank you, Father God, as you prepare to make this world a better place to live in the nearest future.

AUGUST 18

Revelation 22:14

Blessed are they that do his commandments, that they may have right to the tree of life, and may enter in through the gates into the city.

We will obey His commandments, we shall have right to the tree of life, and we will enter into the city of our God. We thank you, Holy Spirit, for helping us see beyond this present world.

AUGUST 19

Isaiah 55:1

Ho, everyone that thirsteth, come ye to the waters, and he that hath no money; come ye, buy and eat: yea come, buy wine and milk without money and without price.

Father God, the owner of silver, gold, diamond, and all kinds and types of money. Thank you for giving us money to spend each passing day as we make transactions with them.

AUGUST 20

Psalm 113:3

From the rising of the sun unto the going down of the same the LORD'S name is to be praised.

It is a Blissful day indeed. Have you said "thank you, Jesus" today? Say it louder and louder, bigger, and bigger. THANK YOU, JESUS CHRIST. From the sun's rising till its setting, we shall continue to thank you and praise you.

AUGUST 21

Psalm 34:22

*The LORD redeemeth the soul of his servants: and
none of them that trust in Him shall be desolate.*

I will exalt you, Lord, You have redeemed my
soul from destruction, and you have lifted me
up. I trust in you, so I shall not be desolated. No
one trust in you shall be desolated. We will
trust in you.

AUGUST 22

Isaiah 66:1

Thus saith the LORD, the heaven is my throne, and the earth is my footstool: ...

Worthy and praise are for you, my Father in heaven, as you made the earth your footstool and the heavens your throne. Your knowledge is unsearchable. Thank you, Father.

AUGUST 23

Psalm 28:7

The LORD is my strength and my shield; my heart trusted in him, and I am helped: therefore my heart greatly rejoiceth; and with my song will I praise thee.

Thank you, Jesus Christ. You have been our strength, our shield, our helper, and our joy. Our hearts rejoice in you. We praise your Name. Amen.

AUGUST 24

Romans 5:1

Therefore being justified by faith, we have peace with God through our Lord Jesus Christ.

Praise and honor be unto you Jesus Christ, the Savior, the Redeemer, and our Justifier giving us peace.

~ GIVE THANKS ALL THE YEAR ROUND ~

AUGUST 25

Genesis 32:10

I am not worthy of the least of all the mercies, and of all the truth, which thou hast shew unto thy servant; for with my staff I passed over this Jordan; and now I am become two bands.

To God be the glory, great things He has been doing in our lives. What great thing can you reflect on today?

AUGUST 26

Nahum 1:9

What do ye imagine against the LORD? He will make an utter end: affliction shall not rise up the second time.

Great and excellent is your work in our lives. We will praise you, worship you and adore you all our days.

AUGUST 27

Luke 1:30

And the Angel said unto her, Fear not, Mary: for thou hast found favour with God.

Thank you, Father, Son, and Holy Spirit, for the beautiful earth and all the beautiful things around us, for the good news we hear time and time again.

AUGUST 28

Genesis 1:25

And God made the beast of the earth after his kind, and cattle after their kinds, and everything that creepeth upon the earth after his kind: and God saw that it was good.

Thank you, Lord, for creating all the beautiful things around the world to make men and women comfortable. This is your doing, and it is marvelous in our sight.

AUGUST 29

Isaiah 27:13

And it shall come to pass in that day, that the great trumpet shall be blown,... and shall worship the LORD in the holy mount at Jerusalem.

Praises and Worship ascribe to you, oh Lord. Thank you, Jesus, for who you are and for all the good things you are doing in our lives, all the earth to worship you.

AUGUST 30

2 Thessalonians 1:3

We are bound to thank God always for you, brethren, as it is meet, because that your faith groweth exceedingly...

Second, to the last day of August, we praise your name, dear Lord, and thank you so much. For making our faith grow in You.

AUGUST 31

Psalm 48:14

For this God is our God for ever and ever: he will be our guide even unto death.

Last day of the month. Praise the Lord! You are our God. You have guided us through the perils and the dangers of the month — and You will guide us through the perilous times.

SEPTEMBER

9/11 has been a memorial in the United States of America. Praying such will not happen again. If you want to know more about September 11, go to the history book. Welcome to the ninth month, pregnancy month, and month of joy.

This month I will take you through one chapter from the book of Psalms.

SEPTEMBER 1

Psalms 136:1

O give thanks unto the LORD: for he is good: for his mercy endureth for ever.

Praise the Lord almighty. It is another new month again. Our God has been good to us, and His love endures forever.

SEPTEMBER 2

Psalm 136:2

O give thanks unto the God of gods: for his mercy endureth for ever.

As we enter into the last quarter of the year, all praise and adoration be unto Jesus Christ, the son of the living God.

SEPTEMBER 3

Psalms 136:3

O give thanks to the Lord of lords for his mercy endureth for ever.

Give thanks to God. He is the Lord over all, the Sovereign God. His Lordship has no end, and His Kingdom is eternal. Thank you, our Father, and our God.

SEPTEMBER 4

Psalms 136:4

To him who alone doeth great wonders: for his mercy endureth for ever.

God alone does great wonders. Thank Him for all the wonders He had done for you, your family, and your ministry.

SEPTEMBER 5

Psalm 136:5

To him that by wisdom made the heavens: for his mercy endureth for ever.

Give God thanks, by His understanding, He made the heavens, not one heaven or two but numerous, wonderful, and glorious heavens.

SEPTEMBER 6

Psalms 136:6

To him that stretched out the earth above the waters: for his mercy endureth for ever.

Give thanks to God for spreading the earth upon the water. Do you know how He did it? Can you explain it? Ah! Worthy are you, oh Lord!

SEPTEMBER 7

Psalms 136:7

To him that made great lights: for his mercy endureth for ever.

Praise the Lord. A week has gone by today. He made the great lights because He dwells in light, and darkness cannot comprehend His light.

SEPTEMBER 8

Psalm 136:8

The sun to rule by day: for his mercy endureth for ever.

Give thanks to God, for He made the sun to shine upon both good and bad, friend and foe, and the sun to rule the day.

SEPTEMBER 9

Psalm 136:9

The moon and stars to rule by night: for his mercy endureth for ever.

Give thanks to God. He has not allowed us to stumble at night and in the dark periods of our lives by providing the light of the moon and stars. And the light of His words during trials and challenges of life.

SEPTEMBER 10

Malachi 3:8.

Will a man rob God? Yet ye have robbed me. But ye say, wherein have we robbed thee? In tithes and offering.

Give God praise and worship for His command of ten percent (10%) of our increase and giving us ninety percent (90%).

SEPTEMBER 11

Psalm 136: 10-11

To him that smote Egypt... and brought out Israel among them: for his mercy endureth for ever.

Give God praise, honor, and glory. The creator of the universe for bringing us out of our physical and spiritual bondage.

SEPTEMBER 12

Psalm 136:12

With a strong hand, and with a stretch out arm: for his mercy endureth for ever.

Give God praise for His Mighty and outstretched arm that has saved us from hell and perdition.

SEPTEMBER 13

Psalm 136:13

To him which divided the Red Sea into parts: for his mercy endureth for ever.

Thank you, Holy Spirit, for making us know the Only, wise God and Jesus Christ — His son who has divided and parted the Red Sea for our sake.

SEPTEMBER 14

Psalm 136:14

And made Israel to pass through the midst of it: for his mercy endureth for ever.

Give thanks to the Lord who has brought His people out of destruction. His grace and mercy endureth forever.

SEPTEMBER 15

Psalm 136:15

But over threw Pharaoh and his host in the Red Sea:
for his mercy endureth for ever.

Thank you, Father God, for sweeping away our sorrows, pains, aches, agony, discomfort, and all negatives into the Red Sea and never to see them again.

SEPTEMBER 16

Psalm 136:16

*To him which led his people through the wilderness:
for his mercy endureth for ever.*

Thank you, Jesus Christ, for great is your name
in our lives doing wonders as you led us
through the desert of the world.

~ GIVE THANKS ALL THE YEAR ROUND ~

SEPTEMBER 17

Psalm 136:17.

To him which smote great kings: for his mercy endureth for ever.

Thank you, Father God, for striking down all our enemies and consuming them all for your name's sake. They shall rise no more.

SEPTEMBER 18

Psalm 136:18.

And slew famous kings: for his mercy endureth for ever.

Today, glory and honor be unto you our Lord, for you are the supreme God, mightier, stronger, and powerful than all the mighty kings of the earth.

SEPTEMBER 19

Psalms 136:19

Sihon king of of the Amorites: for his mercy endureth for ever.

Thank you, Jesus Christ, for reigning in our lives as King for your mercy endures forever. Glory to God in the highest.

SEPTEMBER 20

Psalms 136:20

And Og the king of Bashan: for his mercy endureth for ever.

There is absolutely no one like you, oh Lord among the gods and kings, you are the supper one — the supreme God.

SEPTEMBER 21

Psalm 136:21

And gave their lands for an heritage: for his mercy endureth for ever.

Giving God thanks for giving us the land of the enemies to possess and to dwell peacefully. Take all the glory, oh Lord!

SEPTEMBER 22

Psalms 136:22

Even an heritage unto Israel his servant: for his mercy endureth for ever.

Giving you all the praise due to you, O God, for inheriting us and giving us an inheritance.

SEPTEMBER 23

Psalms 136:23

Who remembered us in our low estate: for his mercy endureth for ever.

Blessings, honor, and adoration to you, the only true and enduring forever God, who always remember us in our low estates.

SEPTEMBER 24

Psalm 136:24

And hath redeemed us from our enemies: for his mercy endureth for ever.

Holy Spirit, we worship you for who you are and for what you are doing and how you've redeemed us, giving us peace and rest of mind.

SEPTEMBER 25

Psalms 136:25

Who giveth food to all flesh: for his mercy endureth for ever.

Thank you, daddy, for giving us food and giving food to all and every creature of yours every day. Awesome, are you always.

SEPTEMBER 26

Psalm 136:26.

O give thanks unto the God of heaven: for his mercy endureth for ever.

Give thanks and praise to God who reigns in heaven and on earth. The unquestionable God who reigns forever.

~ GIVE THANKS ALL THE YEAR ROUND ~

SEPTEMBER 27

Psalms 135:5

For I know that the LORD is great, and that our Lord is above all gods.

Thanking you always, Lord, you are the savior of mankind, the greatest one, the only one, and the Lord above all.

SEPTEMBER 28

1 John 5:7

For there are three that bear record in heaven, the Father, the Word, and the Holy Ghost: and these three are one.

Giving you thanks as you have commanded. You do what pleases you on earth and in the heavens. We thank you for the unity and oneness between the Father, the Word, and the Holy Spirit.

SEPTEMBER 29

Psalms 134: 1-2

Behold, bless ye the LORD, all ye servants of the LORD, which by night stand in the house of the LORD. Lift up your hands in the sanctuary, and bless the LORD.

Let all His servants, ministry workers, choirs, ushers, prayer warriors, evangelists, children's department, welfare department, board of elders, board of trustees, and all God's children give Him praise and lavish Him with thanksgiving. Are you one of His children? Today you can become one as you start praising Him.

SEPTEMBER 30

Psalm 134: 3.

The LORD that made heaven and earth bless thee out of Zion.

Hallelujah, it is the last day of the month, our God omnipotent reigns, the Lord, the maker of heaven and earth. Blessed be thy name. Give Him quality and quantity praise.

OCTOBER

This is a particular month, the month of endless blessings. Welcome to the new month and the tenth month. Remember God requires 10% of all you have, all you do, all you possess, and all your time. The grace of God is sufficient for you. Amen

OCTOBER 1

Psalm 30:1

I will extol thee, O LORD; for thou hast lifted me up, and hast not made my foes to rejoice over me.

Praise the Lord Almighty, my month of celebration. My month of vacation. My month of moving higher and my month of good news. I will extol thee, O Lord, for thou have lifted me up...

OCTOBER 2

Psalm 30:2

O LORD my God, I cried unto thee, and thou hast healed me.

Thank you, Lord, for you are our sanctifier and our healer. You gave us divine healing and divine health. You heal us from all diseases, sicknesses, infirmities. You heard our cry, and you listened to our prayers. Glory!

OCTOBER 3

Psalm 30:3

O LORD thou hast brought up my soul from the grave: thou hast kept me alive, that I should not go down to the pit.

Thank you, Lord, for the gift of life, for the air we breathe in and out, for the purified oxygen that works in our body system.

OCTOBER 4

Psalm 30:4

Sing unto the LORD, O ye saints of his, and give thanks at the remembrance of his holiness.

As I remember your holiness today, I say thank you, Jesus. Let His saints sing unto Him, let them give Him thanks today, and remember how Holy He is.

OCTOBER 5

Psalm 30:12

...O LORD my God, I will give thanks unto thee for ever.

O Lord my God, I will give you thanks and praises forever. The sustainer of our lives. We love you, Lord.

OCTOBER 6

Psalm 28:8

The LORD is their strength, and he is the saving strength of his anointed.

Thank you, Lord, You've been our strength, and you are the strength of those who put their trust in you. And Lord, you are the saving strength of your anointed ones.

OCTOBER 7

Psalm 23:1

The LORD is my shepherd; I shall not want.

Thank you, Jesus Christ. Our good shepherd and the shepherd of our soul. We shall not go astray again from you.

~ GIVE THANKS ALL THE YEAR ROUND ~

OCTOBER 8

Psalm 23:2

He maketh me to lie down in green pastures: he leadeth me beside the still waters.

You are the Lord who made me lie down in green pastures. You led me beside the still waters. I say thank you, Lord.

OCTOBER 9

Psalm 23:3

He restoreth my soul: he leadeth me in the paths of righteousness for his name's sake.

Thank you, Lord Jesus, for restoring my soul and leading me into the path of righteousness. You are the Leader, and I will follow.

OCTOBER 10

Psalm 23:4

Yea, though I walk through the valley of the shadow of death, I will fear no evil: for thou art with me; ...

Thank you, Father God, for being with me in the valley of the shadow of death. No fear can hold me down.

OCTOBER 11

Psalm 23:4

...For thy rod and thy staff, they comfort me.

Thank you, Lord God. Your rod and staff are those that comfort me. Your word and its promises comfort us. We love you, Father God.

OCTOBER 12

John 8:32

And ye shall know the truth, and the truth shall make you free.

Thank you, Lord, for saving my soul. Thank you, Lord, for giving me thy salvation so true and free. We know the truth, for you are the truth. Since we know you, the truth has made us free.

OCTOBER 13

Psalm 23:5

Thou preparest a table before me in the presence of my enemies: ...

Thank you, Our Father, you prepared a table before us in the presence of our enemies. We thank you for preparing a table before us at the rapture of the saints. We hope for this glorious day.

OCTOBER 14

Psalm 23:5

...Thou anointest my head with oil; my cup runneth over.

Thank you, Father God, you anoint my head and my whole body inside out. My cup now runs over. Praise the Lord for this great anointing.

OCTOBER 15

Psalm 23:6

Surely goodness and mercy shall follow me all the days of my life: and I will dwell in the house of LORD for ever. Amen

Thank you, Lord, for making your goodness and mercy follow me all my life and causing me to dwell in your house forever.

OCTOBER 16

Psalm 150:6

Let everything that hath breath praise the LORD.
Praise ye the LORD.

Give thanks to the Lord of lords and King of
kings and let everything that hath breath praise
the Lord.

OCTOBER 17

John 3:16

For God so loved the world, that he gave his only begotten Son, that whosoever believeth in him should not perish, but have everlasting life.

Glory to God Almighty for His love over and around us. Thank you, Jesus Christ, for your love that brings salvation. We cannot do without you, Lord.

OCTOBER 18

Matthew 27:51

And behold, the veil of the temple was rent in Twain from the top to the bottom:...

This God shall be our God forever. Thank you, Jesus, for giving us access to God the Father.

OCTOBER 19

Matthew 27:52

And the graves were opened; and many bodies of the saints which slept arose.

H-A-L-L-E-L-U-J-A-H.

You are the God of our fathers, the creator of heaven and earth. The resurrection and the life. Praises and worship be unto you.

OCTOBER 20

Psalm 13:6

I will sing unto the LORD, because he hath dealt bountifully with me.

Another wonderful day to bless and to give thanks. Lord Jesus, you that deals with us bountifully, we say thank you.

OCTOBER 21

Mark 6:31

*And he said unto them, Come ye yourselves apart
into a desert place and rest a while.*

God said, come apart for a while and rest.
Thank you for giving us divine rest. Please take
time off and rest, take a vacation, be with your
family, have time with your family, and rest.

OCTOBER 22

Matthew 9:36

But when he saw the multitude, he was moved with compassion on them, because they fainted, and were scattered abroad, as sheep having no shepherd.

Blessed be the name of the Lord Almighty. His love and compassion never fail. We will not be frail, scattered, nor scared, for we have a good shepherd.

323

OCTOBER 23

1 Corinthians 13:4

Charity (Love) suffereth long, and it's kind: charity envieth not: charity vaunteth not itself, is not puff up.

Thank you, Jesus, you love me too much, yes you love all, but mine is exceptional. Hallelujah! Thank you, Jesus Christ. Do you know that the love of God towards you is also exceptional?

OCTOBER 24

1 Thessalonians 5:18

In everything give thanks: for this is the will of God in Christ Jesus concerning you.

Thank you, Jesus Christ, for strengthening us even in overwhelming situations and making it easy to move on always.

OCTOBER 25

Psalm 28:7-8

The LORD is my strength and my shield; my heart trusted in him, and I am helped: therefore my heart greatly rejoiceth; and with my song will I praise Him.

Lord, you are too much in your endless blessings and limitless grace. Thank you, Jesus Christ, forever I will be grateful. Today is a special day to remember, praise, worship, and adore the only wise God. Thank You.

OCTOBER 26

Hebrews 2:9

Thou hast loved righteousness, and hate iniquity;
therefore God, even thy God, hath anointed thee with
the oil of gladness above thy fellows.

Father God, we give you all the glory and honor
for all your wondrous works. You hate
iniquities, and you love righteousness. Thank
you for the oil of gladness.

OCTOBER 27

Jonah 4:6

And the LORD God prepared a gourd, and made it to come up over Jonah, that it might be a shadow over his head, to deliver him from his grief. So, Jonah was exceeding glad of the gourd.

It was a surprise blessing from the Lord today. Did you receive a surprise package? Give Him praise. Thank you, Jesus.

OCTOBER 28

Acts 8:35

Then Philip opened his mouth, and began at the same scripture, and preached unto him JESUS.

Thank you, the God of heaven and earth, for giving us JESUS CHRIST to save sinners from destruction. We thank You.

OCTOBER 29

Hebrews 2:12-13

Saying, I will declare thy name unto my brethren, in the midst of the church will I sing praise unto thee. And again I will put my trust in him. And again, Behold I and the children which God hath given me.

Worthy is your name, oh Lord. Today, we are thankful for all your benefits over our lives, families, and the ministry. Receive our thanks.

OCTOBER 30

Matthew 28: 8

And they departed quickly from the sepulchre with fear and great joy; and did run to bring his disciples word.

Hallelujah! Victory is won, success is won, and we have overcome. Praise the Lord. Thank you, dear Lord.

OCTOBER 31

Genesis 17:5, 15; Acts 13:9

Neither shall thy name any more be called Abram, but thy name shall be Abraham... As for Sarai thy wife, thou shalt not call her name Sarai, but Sarah shall her name be. Then Saul, (who also is called Paul), filled with the Holy Ghost, set his eyes on him.

To God be the glory, for today is the last day of the month. As God changed these people's lives and changed their names, so shall this day be changed to HALLELUJAH NIGHT. Thank you, Jesus, for this day is known as Hallelujah Night. Praise God!

NOVEMBER

This is the month of thanksgiving to the Lord. It is also the month of harvest. We shall all have reasons to be thankful to God all the days of our lives in Jesus Christ Mighty Name. Amen

NOVEMBER 1

Psalm 92:5

O LORD, how great are thy works! and thy thoughts are very deep.

Great are you, Lord, and greatly to be praised. You have been from ages to ages, and you have deep thoughts towards us. Thank you, Father.

NOVEMBER 2

Revelation 21:3

And I heard a great voice out of heaven saying, Behold, the tabernacle of God is with men, and he will dwell with them, and they shall be his people, and God himself shall be with them, and be their God. Amen

For this God shall be our God forever. Hallelujah! Glory! We are your people, and you are our God. Thank you, Jesus.

NOVEMBER 3

Revelation 21:4

*And God shall wipe away all tears from their eyes;
and there shall be no more death, neither sorrow, nor
crying, neither shall there be any more pain: for the
former things are passed away.*

Thank you, Father God, for wiping away our
tears, our sorrows, and our groaning. Your
word says there shall no more be pain, sorrow,
crying, and death. We believe your Word, and
we give You praise.

NOVEMBER 4

Revelation 21:7

*He that overcometh shall inherit all things; and I
will be his God, and he shall be my son.*

Jesus Christ, through your blood that was shed
on the cross, you made us become overcomers.
We give you thanks.

NOVEMBER 5

1 John 1:5

This is the message which we have heard of him, and declare unto you, that God is light, and in him is no darkness at all.

Thank you, Jesus Christ—you are our light and the light of the world. Darkness cannot comprehend this light. We thank you for the message of light.

NOVEMBER 6

Jeremiah 31:35

Thus saith the LORD, which giveth the sun for a light by day, and the ordinances of the moon and of the stars for a light by night, which divideth the sea when the waves thereof roar; The LORD of host is his name:

Thank you, Father God, for taking care of us and for your manifold blessings. You are always there for us in stormy, scary, and scared seasons of our time and the weather.

NOVEMBER 7

John 8:42

Jesus said unto them, if God were your Father, ye would love me: for I proceeded forth and came from God; neither came I of myself, but he sent me.

Every day of my life, will I give you praise and worship, for I am proud of you as my Father and my God.

NOVEMBER 8

Romans 4:17

(As it is written, I have made thee a father of many nations) before him whom he believed, even God, who quickeneth the dead, and calleth those things which be not as though they were.

Thank you, Lord, for your promise to make me a father of nations. Claim this promise for yourself.

NOVEMBER 9

Exodus 15:2

The LORD is my strength and song, and he is become my salvation: he is my God, and I will prepare him an habitation; my father's God and I will exalt him.

You are my Father, and you have become my God. I have prepared my body to be your habitation. Thank you, Lord. Beloved, you too, can start preparing yourself for His habitation so that his coming will not meet us unawares.

NOVEMBER 10

Ezra 7:27

Blessed be the LORD God of our fathers, which hath put such thing as this in the king's heart, to beautify the house of the LORD...

Blessed be the Lord God of Host and our father for beautifying our body as your temple. Thank you, Jesus Christ.

NOVEMBER 11

Psalm 27:10

*When my father and my mother forsake me, then the
LORD will take me up.*

Thank you, Jesus, for when our father and
mother forsake us, you have been there as our
eternal Father.

NOVEMBER 12

Psalm 68:5

A Father of the fatherless, and a judge of the widows, is God in his Holy habitations.

Thank you, Lord Jesus, for being the advocate and Judge to the poor, the needy, and the orphans to rescue them from being oppressed. Glory to your name.

NOVEMBER 13

Matthew 26:27

And he took the cup, and gave thanks, and gave it them saying, Drink ye all of it.

Give thanks to the only one God. Give thanks because Jesus Christ gave us himself, the only begotten son of God. Give thanks.

NOVEMBER 14

1 Corinthians 1:4

I thank my God always on your behalf, for the grace of God which is giving you by Jesus Christ.

Lord, I thank you on behalf of my family (both biological and spiritual children), friends, co-workers, and brethren. They are all for you now and forever. Amen.

NOVEMBER 15

2 Thessalonians 1:3

We are bound to thank God always for you, brethren, as it is meet, because that your faith groweth exceedingly, and the charity of every one of you all towards each other aboundeth.

Lord, we are thankful to you for making our faith grow exceedingly and for your love that binds the believers together.

NOVEMBER 16

Psalm 128:2

For thou shall eat the labor of thine hands: happy shalt thou be, and it shall be well with thee. Amen

Thank you, Father God, for the promise of eating the fruits of my labor. I shall not die young, or prematurely, or suddenly, or accidentally. We shall not die the death of another person. Amen.

NOVEMBER 17

Isaiah 3:10

Say ye to the righteous, that it shall be well with him: for they shall eat the fruit of their doings.

Thank you, Jesus Christ, for it is well with me, my family, ministry, and all that concerns me. Amen

NOVEMBER 18

1 Corinthians 15:57

But thanks be to God, which giveth us the victory through our Lord Jesus Christ.

Thanks be to our God, who has given us the daily victory through our Lord Jesus Christ. Victory over Sin, Satan, Flesh, and over all our Enemies.

NOVEMBER 19

Genesis 1:1

In the beginning God created the heaven and the earth.

Thank you, Father God, for our nation and our land. The heavens and the earth belong to you. You created them, and they are all yours.

NOVEMBER 20

Ezekiel 34:26

And I will make them and the places round about my hill a blessing: and I will cause the shower to come down in its season; there shall be showers of blessing.

Giving thanks to God is in my blood. You did it, Lord. Thank you for your manifold blessings and for nonseasonal showers of blessings.

NOVEMBER 21

John 14:16,26

And I will pray the Father, and he shall give you another Comforter, that he may abide with you for ever; But the Comforter, which is the Holy Ghost, whom the Father will send in my name, he shall teach you all things, and bring all things to your remembrance, whatsoever I have said unto you.

Thank you, Holy Spirit, the third in the Godhead, for comforting us, teaching us and instructing us, making us remember what the Lord had said.

NOVEMBER 22

Ephesians 1:5

Having predestined us unto the adoption of children by Jesus Christ to himself, according to the good pleasure of His will.

Thank you, Holy Spirit, for giving us the power to experience adoption and to be a witness of the Faith.

~ GIVE THANKS ALL THE YEAR ROUND ~

NOVEMBER 23

Proverbs 4:23

Keep thy heart with all diligence for out of it are the issues of life.

Thank you, Holy Spirit, for saving us from destruction and keeping our hearts diligently.

NOVEMBER 24

Psalm 56:4 & 11

In God I will praise his word, in God I have put my trust; I will not fear what flesh can do unto me. In God have I put my trust: I will not be afraid what man can do unto me.

Thank you, Lord, for making me trust in you through your Holy Spirit and for making us overcome the flesh.

NOVEMBER 25

Psalm 59:1

Deliver me from my enemies, O my God; defend me from them that rise up against me.

Our defender, we thank you. You delivered us from our enemies, both physical and spiritual enemies. You defended us from our accusers, and you defeated them all.

NOVEMBER 26

Psalm 61:1

Hear my cry O God; attend to unto my prayer.

Thank you, Father God, for hearing our cry and attending to our prayers always through your Holy Spirit.

NOVEMBER 27

Psalm 51:7

Purge me with hyssop, and I shall be clean: wash me and I shall be whiter than snow.

Holy Spirit, we worship you, using the blood of the Lamb shed on the cross to clean and purge us from all our unrighteousness. We cannot thank you enough.

NOVEMBER 28

Psalm 66:1-2

Make a joyful noise unto God, all ye lands: sing forth the honor of his name: make his praise glorious.

Holy Spirit, we thank you for making a joyful noise in us unto the Lord. Our land will sing songs that will honor your name. Musicians, at the amusement parks, at the cinema theaters, we will proclaim your name.

NOVEMBER 29

Matthew 12:32

And whosever speaketh a word against the Son of man, it shall be forgiven him: but whosoever speaketh against the Holy Ghost, it shall not be forgiven him, neither in this world, neither in the world to come.

Holy Spirit, the third in the Trinity, blessings and honor, be ascribed unto you now and forever. We shall not speak against you but embrace you.

NOVEMBER 30

Luke 9:23

And he said to them all, If any man will come after me, let him deny himself, and take up his cross daily, and follow me.

It is the last day of the month, Glory! Hallelujah! Praise and Honor be unto you, our God. Thank you, Father, Son, and Holy Spirit, for empowering us to carry our cross and follow you daily. We shall not look back in Jesus' Name. Amen

DECEMBER

The month that completes the year the Christmas month. The beginning and the end month. Thank you, Father God, from January to December. You are great, you are wonderful, you are awesome, Lord.

DECEMBER 1

Revelation 1:8

I am Alpha and Omega, the beginning and the ending, saith the Lord, which is, and which was, and which is to come, the Almighty.

Today is the beginning of the last month of the year. The Alpha and the Omega, the beginning and the end, you are much appreciated.

DECEMBER 2

Isaiah 45:7

I formed the light, and created darkness: I made peace and created evil: I the LORD do all these things.

Thank you, Father God. The only wise God who formed the light and created darkness, who made peace and created evil, the good and the bad. Worthy are you, oh Lord.

DECEMBER 3

1 Timothy 1:12

And I thank Christ Jesus our Lord, who hath enabled me, for that he counted me faithful, putting me into the ministry.

Thank you, Jesus, for counting us faithful and putting us into the ministry. Therefore the ministry will thrive and prosper. We praise you, Lord Jesus.

DECEMBER 4

1 Chronicles 23:30

And to stand every morning to thank and praise the LORD, and likewise at even;

Every morning will I say thanks and praise You, Lord. Even in the evening and at midnight, your praises will never cease from my mouth.

DECEMBER 5

Daniel 2:23

I thank thee, and praise thee, O thou God of my fathers who hast given me wisdom and might, and hast made known unto me now what we desired of thee: ...

Thank you, Lord, for giving us wisdom, strength, and might to do our daily jobs and activities. As we step out today, we will come back and say: El-Elohe-Israel, meaning "Arrived Safely." (Genesis 33:20)

369

DECEMBER 6

Romans 6:17-18

But God be thanked, that ye were the servants of sin, but ye have obeyed from the heart that form of doctrine which was delivered you. Being then made free from sin, ye become the servants of righteousness.

Thank You, Jesus, for we are no more under the yoke of the sin of unbelief, but you made us believe in you and made us become the servants of righteousness.

DECEMBER 7

Ephesians 5:20

Giving thanks always for all things unto God and the Father in the name of our Lord Jesus Christ.

We give thanks to God always for all things and for everything you have done in our lives. Today makes one week of this last month. Sit down and ponder on what the Lord has done for you. Just think of one thing and give him thanks.

DECEMBER 8

1 Thessalonians 3:9

For what thanks can we render to God again for you, for all the joy wherewith we joy for your sakes before our God:

Lord, we thank you for the joy of salvation. This joy will abide with us forever. We thank you, Lord, for the joy of life you gave us. And for everything.

DECEMBER 9

Revelation 4:9

*And when those beasts give glory and honor and
thanks to him that sat on the throne, who liveth for
ever and ever.*

Thank you, Lord God, you created us as human
beings and not as beasts. Both man and beast
will give you praise. You live and reign forever.

DECEMBER 10

Nehemiah 11:17

And Mattaniah the son of Micha, the son of Zabdi, the son of Asaph was the principal to begin the thanksgiving in prayer: ....

Today is a day of thanksgiving, and nothing will hold us back. Thank you, Jesus Christ. We have made ourselves available as the principal vessel to begin the thanksgiving prayer.

DECEMBER 11

Nehemiah 12:8

Moreover, the Levites: Jeshua, Binnui, Kadmiel, Sherniah, which was over the thanksgiving, he and his brethren.

My family, both at home and abroad, the Church of God, we are all thankful to you, God—for your manifold blessings to every one of us.

DECEMBER 12

2 Corinthians 4:15

For all things are for your sakes, that the abundant grace might through the thanksgiving of many redound to the glory of God.

Let our thanksgiving be unto the Lord for his glory that he will never share with anyone. We will praise you forever.

DECEMBER 13

2 Corinthians 9:11

Being enriched in every thing to all bountifulness,
which causeth through us thanksgiving to God.

Thank you, Father God, for enriching us in
everything. Making us complete and abound in
all heavenly riches and blessings.

DECEMBER 14

Psalm 26:7

That I may publish with the voice of thanksgiving, and tell of all thy wondrous works.

Yes, Lord! You are great and glorious. Thank you, Jesus Christ, I will publish with the voice of thanksgiving of your Holy Name in all the earth.

DECEMBER 15

Psalm 95:2

Let us come to his presence with thanksgiving, and make a joyful noise unto him with psalms.

Giving Him praise and thanks all our days as we come to His presence daily, making a joyful noise unto our God with psalms. Please, make a joyful noise unto the Lord.

DECEMBER 16

Isaiah 51:3

For the LORD shall comfort Zion: he will comfort all her waste places; and he will make her wilderness like Eden, and her desert like the garden of the LORD; joy and gladness shall be found therein, thanksgiving, and the voice of melody.

Thank you, Lord, for turning our mourning into dancing, joy, and rejoicing. Absolutely, there is a melody in our hearts.

DECEMBER 17

Amos 4:5

And offer a sacrifice of thanksgiving with leaven,
and proclaim and publish the free offering...

I will not lack or slack in giving you thanks.
Thank you, Jesus Christ, my Savior. Accept my
free offering today and always.

DECEMBER 18

Philippians 4:6

Be careful for nothing; but in everything by prayer and supplication with thanksgiving let your request be made known unto God.

Giving thanksgiving is a requirement for a victorious Christian life and for answered prayers. Thank you, Jesus.

~ GIVE THANKS ALL THE YEAR ROUND ~

DECEMBER 19

Colossians 4:2

Continue in prayer, and watch in the same with thanksgiving;

Praying and watching in thanksgiving to the only wise, eternal God, who is always ready to listen and to answer us. All your responses to our prayers (Yes, No, Wait) are good for our well-being. Thank you, Lord.

DECEMBER 20

Psalm 66:4

All the earth shall worship thee, and shall sing unto thee; they shall sing to thy name. Selah.

Thank you, Father, of all fathers, King of all kings, You are worthy of my praise for all the earth shall worship and praise you.

DECEMBER 21

Psalm 139:14

I will praise thee; for I am fearfully and wonderfully made: marvelous are thy works; and that my soul knoweth right well.

God, thank you for your creativity and artistic works. You created humans in black, white, brown, yellow, tall, short, fat, lean, eloquent, stammerer, blind, deaf, poor, rich, etc., for your pleasure. Help us to reflect on them today and always.

DECEMBER 22

Psalm 91:1

He that dwelleth in the secret place of the most High shall abide under the shadow of the Almighty.

Father God, we thank you, keeping us safe in the hollow of your hands. Today and always, we shall abide under the shadow of Almighty.

DECEMBER 23

Matthew 6:26, 28

Behold the fowls of the air: for they sow not, neither do they reap, nor gather into barns...... Consider the lilies of the field, how they grow; they toil not, neither do they spin:
(Read Matthew 6:24-34 for more gems).

Almighty Father, thank you for creating me into this beautiful world and making me impact your creativity of human beings, animals in the jungles, fishes in the oceans, birds of the air, and tinny insects. The plants, the flowers, the fruits, and vegetables.

DECEMBER 24

John 1:12

But as many as received him, to them gave he power to become the sons of God, even to them that believe on his name.

Thank you, Father God, for giving us your only begotten son for our redemption and for giving us the power of adoption. We praise your Holy Name.

DECEMBER 25

Matthew 1:21

And she shall bring forth a son, and thou shalt call his name JESUS: for he shall save his people from their sins.

Christ is born Glory to God in the highest. Peace on earth. Thank you, Jesus, the Savior, for coming into our world to redeem mankind in whom I am one.

DECEMBER 26

Psalm 48:10

According to thy name, O God, so is thy praise unto the ends of the earth: thy right hand is full of righteousness.

The praise of our God raised up from the center of our heart to heaven. Glory be to Your Holy Name.

DECEMBER 27

Lamentations 3:25

The LORD is good unto them that wait for him, to the soul that seeketh him.

I will sing of the mercies of the Lord, for by your mercy we are not consumed. You are good to us as we wait patiently for your promises.

DECEMBER 28

Psalm 103:1

Praise the LORD, O my soul: and all that is within me, bless his holy name.

Let all that is in me praise the name of the Lord. Your praise and thanksgiving are my daily bread.

DECEMBER 29

Ecclesiastes 3:11

He hath made everything beautiful in his time...

Father God, thank You for the beautiful weather. Thank You for the birds that sing, waves of the tree, and natural air that we breathe in and out. It's all the beautiful works of your hand.

DECEMBER 30

Revelation 22:13

I am Alpha and Omega, the beginning and the end, the first and the last.

Praise the name of the Lord. From the beginning of your life to the ending, He is the Alfa and the omega, the beginning and the end of all things.

DECEMBER 31

Revelation 22:7

Behold, I come quickly: blessed is he that keepeth the sayings of the prophecy of this book.

Thanking God for He has been, He is, and He is our coming King, He is the same yesterday, today, tomorrow, and till eternity.

P-R-A-I-S-E the LORD!

Last day of the month and of the year. Glory to God in the highest, for we shall all see the new year joyfully.

~ GIVE THANKS ALL THE YEAR ROUND ~

Happy New Year in Advance!

As you are preparing to enter the new year joyfully, my prayer is that you will have every reason to give God thanks all the year round and give Him thanks all the days of your life until we all see Christ in all his glory. Amen. Thank you for using this book as your daily devotional.

Made in the USA
Middletown, DE
20 January 2022